the scottish play

Polyam Fam

Book One

phoebe alexander

MOUNTAINS WANTED
PUBLISHING & INDIE AUTHOR SERVICES

Mountains Wanted Publishing

P.O. Box 50

Harbeson, Delaware 19951

www.mountainswanted.com

Paperback ISBN: 978-1-949394-61-0

Cover photos licensed through Depositphotos

❉ Created with Vellum

To the ones who showed me I had the capacity to love beyond my wildest imagination, and for loving me right back.

one

. . .

molly

"BUT THEY ALL SUCKED!" I ran my fingers through my cotton candy-pink hair in frustration. "And not in a good way."

Jason let out a little chuckle, and I shot him an appreciative nod.

"Thank you! At least *someone* is listening to me." I blew out a breathy sigh of frustration as I looked down at my audition notes, making little checkmarks by the actors I thought might work for speaking parts.

"We're all listening to you," Poe, my girlfriend, assured me. She smirked at her brother, who was the only one to laugh at my *not sucking in a good way* joke. "You're practically shouting. Half of Bloomington is listening to you, Molls."

Jason's girlfriend, Cynda, stood up. "Anyone want something from the kitchen? My wine glass is empty." She pouted and looked down at the empty glass, shaking it a little as if we needed proof.

"Hey, Molly, maybe you should drink a glass—or three." Poe rolled her eyes. She was getting sick of hearing about my play.

The rest of the polycule was too—I had no doubt. "Look, I'm sorry I keep babbling on and on about this, but just think, guys, once we strike the set for this production, that's it! I'm finished! I'll be the proud owner of a Master of Fine Arts degree."

"And we're all very proud of you!" Cynda announced from the kitchen as she stood pouring wine into two glasses. She carried them both into the living room where we were gathered and handed me one. "Here, have a drink, sweetie."

"Have three," Poe chimed in with a smirk. Her cat, Sagan, jumped onto her lap, and she stroked down his long, ginger-colored fur.

"You've been working on this degree for two years now." Cynda sat down on the ottoman, took a sip of her wine and licked her full lips. "You're in the home stretch. You know we're here for you no matter what."

"And, for the record, this production won't be the end of it," Poe pointed out. "It might be the end of your grad school career, but you'll be doing plenty of other productions in the future, won't you?"

"I sure hope so." I sighed again, then took a well-deserved sip of the Moscato Cynda had generously poured for me. "At least I know one play I wrote will get produced. There's no guarantee for any I write after this."

Cynda set her wine glass down and spread her hands as if framing a picture. "I can see it now, a marquis all lit up with the name Molly Rose! It's on Broadway, or maybe it's in Chicago—how does that sound?"

"Thank you for always being so supportive." I smiled at the matriarch of our group.

Poe and I moved in with Cynda and Jason about six months ago when my rent went up so much, I couldn't afford it anymore. Poe was between jobs at the time, and I was a poor grad student who occasionally taught acting workshops for kids at the local community theater. Poe's older brother, Jason, and his girlfriend, Cynda, who was several years older than him, let us move into their three-bedroom house on the west side of Bloomington. So, Cynda became the mother hen of our new little family, some of us related by blood, some of us bonded by love.

"So…question for ya: can you only cast undergrad theater majors?" Poe scratched her chin and looked up at me, the wheels in her mind obviously turning. She was the type of person who loved to solve problems rather than just dwell on how wrong things were going. It was a miracle we got along, to be honest. I could certainly be a dweller.

"I can cast whoever I want, as long as they're okay with not getting paid. It's almost always undergrad theater majors who audition, though sometimes first-year MFA acting students will, just to get a show under their belts. Anything to pad their resumes, you know."

I sighed what was likely my hundredth sigh of the day. "I'm sure things will be okay. I might be acting a bit over-dramatic—"

"Overdramatic!" Poe threw her hands up in the air. "You don't say?!"

Everyone laughed.

Well, I did have a flair for the dramatic, but I was a freaking theater geek through and through. I had basically come out of the womb reciting, "All the world's a stage, and all the men and women merely players." And then, like my hero, Shakespeare, I grew up to be a playwright.

"It's really the male lead I'm having trouble with." Looking down at the audition notes, I shook my head. I couldn't see any of the people who auditioned playing the part of Hamish MacGregor.

"Tell us again what you're looking for?" Jason leaned forward, his elbows on his knees. "Maybe I know a guy?"

"Well, the character is Scottish, hence the name of the play: *Scot Free*. And he's been falsely convicted of murdering his cousin. He escapes from prison and is hiding out in the woods when he meets the main female character, Ruth, who happens to be an attorney."

"That's some pretty damn good luck." Poe shook her head, chuckling. She'd only heard the plot of this play, not to mention every single line, approximately four billion times. I did feel for her. Yes, she could be painfully sarcastic at times, but she was also a saint for putting up with me. Her sarcasm must have been my penance.

"Yeah, I mean he's lucky for meeting her, but he was also framed for murder—so *not* lucky, generally speaking." I shrugged. "Anyway, he's big and gruff and doesn't want her help at first, but he has no choice. He ends up showing his vulnerable side. They fall in love, she tracks down the evidence and gets him off—the charges, I mean—"

"Right," the other three said in unison. Should've expected that from this crew.

"And everyone lives happily ever after!" I finished. "Except the playwright, casting director, executive director and producer—who all happen to be me!"

Poe grabbed the notebook out of my hands and skimmed my notes. Sagan jumped off her lap, deeply offended that she'd moved. His tail twitched when he hit the floor. "So, none of these guys looks like a hulking Scotsman?"

"Um, that would be a no. Most of them are gangly eighteen- and nineteen-year-olds who barely need to shave."

"Right." Poe bit her bottom lip, the way she often did when she was thinking. Then she looked up at me with her crooked grin, her hazel eyes twinkling. "I believe I have an answer to your dilemma."

"You do?" Like I said, she was a problem-solver.

"Do tell," Jason piped up, his eyes settling on the matching set belonging to his sister.

Poe turned her attention back to us after she watched Sagan saunter down the hallway. "Remember when I told you the greenhouse in the biology building is undergoing some renovation? They didn't hire a construction company to do the work—they're handling it in-house. Well, the facilities guy in charge of it is Scottish."

My spine immediately straightened from its formerly slumped posture. *Someone who is already on campus?* "Tell me more…"

"Well, I don't really know him or anything. I've just been in the greenhouse a few times to see the progress. They're building this cool new fountain in the middle of the space. Anyway, I'm *pretty* sure he's Scottish."

Cynda drained her second glass of wine. "What's he look like?"

"Well, he's tall, broad—you know, like a beefy lumberjack kind of guy. Big arms. Big legs. He's got reddish-brown hair. He definitely has an accent—and his name is Lachlan. I read it on his shirt."

"His shirt?" My eyebrows arched.

"Yeah, the facilities guys have their names embroidered on their uniform shirts," Poe explained.

"But you don't know if he has any acting experience?" I stood up, pacing back and forth behind the sofa as I considered this development.

"If he looks the part and has the accent, how hard can the acting part be?" Jason interjected.

I stopped pacing and shot him a glare. He was always trying to rile me up—almost like he was my big brother instead of Poe's. But I wasn't taking the bait. Instead, I wrung my hands as I remembered the half dozen undergrads who'd auditioned for the role of Hamish MacGregor —and how no amount of acting experience could transform any of them into a hulking Scottish beast.

I turned to Poe. "Do you think you could, like, casually ask him if he'd have any interest in playing the leading role in a grad students' thesis project, which would require hours of his time for absolutely zero pay?"

Yeah, it sounds pretty ridiculous when you say it like that, doesn't it?

My girlfriend shrugged. "I mean, I can try. I wouldn't have brought it up if I didn't think it was worth a shot."

"You can be very persuasive." Cynda leaned over to pat Poe on the back.

I started pacing again. "You're right. It's worth a shot. Because right now I've got no clue how I'm going to pull this off. And I only have four weeks. We need to start rehearsals immediately."

Poe walked over to me and swept me into her arms, planting a kiss on my forehead. Easy for her because I was barely five feet tall, and she towered over me at five-feet-eight.

I wrapped my arms around her and laid my head on

her chest, feeling the solid thump of her heart under my ear. I was a lucky woman to have her in my life, and to have her brother and his girlfriend too was a nice bonus. Living in a polycule was the best decision I'd ever made.

"Hey, I gotta go," Poe reminded me, pulling out of our embrace. "Delaney and I are going to go see the eight o'clock showing of *Midnight Killer*."

Cynda's friend Delaney and Poe had hit it off, and they had started to date. We had an open relationship and both considered ourselves to be polyamorous, so I was cool with it. Besides, I hated horror movies, and Poe and Delaney both loved them. Weirdos that they were. So they had that to bond over.

"You'll talk to this Lachlan character tomorrow?" I followed her into our bedroom as she stripped off her shirt. She was apparently changing into a different outfit for her date. Sagan jumped up on the bed to ogle her. He was a pervy cat.

I stood there, just as pervy as the cat, zeroing in on her athletic figure. And for a brief second, I forgot I had asked her a question.

"Hey," she stepped over to me, snapping her fingers in my face, "what's your deal? I said I would talk to him."

"Sorry, I got mesmerized by your tits." I reached out and stroked a finger across her sports bra, then poked it in her cleavage, enjoying the feel of her soft skin.

"Molly, I need to go, sweetheart. I'm running late." She laughed as she stepped out of the way and held up two shirts from her closet. "Gray or black?"

She had a fairly monotone wardrobe. I enjoyed bright colors—hence the pink hair.

"Um, gray?" I shrugged. "No, black. Contrasts with your hair."

She had shoulder-length honey-brown hair and gorgeous hazel eyes with thick lashes that required absolutely zero eye makeup. I was jealous. I had to paint my reddish-blond lashes with a zillion coats of mascara to get any length or volume.

"I figured you'd say that." She leaned over and pecked me on the cheek before she pulled the black V-neck shirt over her head. "You're sure you're okay with me going out tonight? I know you're upset the auditions didn't go as planned…"

"Yes, I'm fine. I'm going to watch the video I shot at auditions and take some more notes. I'll probably be up late. I need to get this cast list out ASAP so we can start practices. We only have the theater for four weeks, you know. There is no time to spare. I realize this Lachlan guy is a total long shot, but I know you can work your magic on him."

She scoffed. "What magic? You know I'm not going to flirt with him." She rolled her eyes. "But *you* can if you want."

"Um, no thanks. I'm into girls." I fluttered my eyelashes at her. "Especially girls like you." I pulled her close to brush my lips against hers. "Knock 'em dead tonight, babe."

Her eyes sparkled as the tiniest smile curled her lips. "Thank you, beautiful. I won't be too late."

She headed out, and I went back to the living room where I'd left my notebook and phone. Cynda and Jason were getting comfy on the sofa, about to watch another episode of *Only Murders in the Building*. If only I could cast my play half as well as that series was cast…

"Have fun, you guys," I called down the hall as I returned to my room to review the audition footage.

The cat gave me the stink-eye when I plopped down next to him. "So, Sagan, do you have any acting experience?"

lachlan

I was tightening the last bolt in the new water feature wall we were building in the biology building's greenhouse when I heard a throat clearing behind me. I turned around to see an average-sized female with brown hair and a face like a pixie. "This area is closed right now, ma'am," I tossed over my shoulder, my words little more than a series of grunts. I was not exactly known for my people skills.

"I know," she tucked her hair behind her ear, "but I need to talk to you."

I set down my wrench and turned around to face her. "What can I do for you?" I struggled to put a neutral expression on my face, as dealing with people was not my favorite pastime. It wasn't my favorite present time or future time either.

"You're Scottish, right?" She looked at me through piercing eyes that felt like they were staring right through me. "Lachlan is a Scottish name, isn't it?"

"I'm Lan or Lanny, if I know you," I corrected.

I hadn't gone by my full first name since I was a kid, and only if my mother was scolding me for something. In general, my family didn't even call me Lachlan—they had a nickname for me that I'd rather not get into right now.

"I see," was all she said, but she remained in place, assessing me.

I cocked my head and swallowed down my growing frustration. "Do you need something?"

She clenched her hands into fists and firmly planted them on her hips. Then her feet spread like she was preparing to stand her ground. It was weird to see her take such a defensive pose, like she was on the rugby pitch at kickoff. Who the hell was this woman, and why was she in my greenhouse?

"I just want to know if you're Scottish." She rolled her eyes.

"*Och aye, lassie, ye ken,*" I shot back in a thick brogue. Then I rolled my eyes right back at her.

A little smirk appeared at the edges of her mouth, and her fists relaxed at her side. "I'm sorry. I should have introduced myself first. I apologize."

"Go on, then." I tilted my head and stared at her.

"I'm Poe Davis, bio admin assistant. It's nice to meet you."

"Likewise." Though "nice" probably wasn't the term I would use. "Now, what can I do for ya, Ms. Davis? I need to get back to work."

"Right." She sucked in a deep breath. "So, you're going to think this is crazy, but—"

I watched her mouth moving, but I wasn't comprehending any of her words. I was more wondering why female folk were always so enamored with my being Scottish. It dawned on me right then that I hadn't been properly leveraging that advantage all this time I'd been over in the States. It never really occurred to me. But dozens of women had commented on my nationality since I'd started work here at the university. There had to be something useful in it, didn't there?

Probably not useful enough to get a green card. But if it got a man laid, well, that would be something, wouldn't it? It had been a while.

"So, what do you think?" Her face exploded into a brilliant smile. She ran a finger through her straight shoulder-length hair and waited expectantly for my response.

"What do I think about what?" I scratched the stubble on my chin.

"About helping a theater grad student out?" She handed me a business card. "This is her info. She has office hours today from three to five. Do you think you could stop by and chat with her about it?"

I sighed. "What kind of help does she need?" I squinted in confusion at Ms. Davis, whose expression immediately twisted in frustration as soon as she heard my question.

"Weren't you listening to me?" She tapped a foot and glared up at me.

"Of course I was."

I wasn't. Clearly.

I looked down at the card and read, *Molly Rose, Graduate Assistant-MFA program. Theater Department Room 204B.*

Something about this Ms. Davis character rubbed me the wrong way, but I couldn't put my finger on it. She was a secretary. The building secretaries were notorious for gossip and causing issues for the facilities folks like myself.

I just smiled and nodded, not wanting to start any type of trouble. Admin assistants and the facilities folks were what kept this campus going—together we were like MacGyver. This place would surely fall apart if not for us.

"Sure, I'll head over there when I get off at four." I waved the card and nodded, hoping that would get rid of her.

"See that you do," was all she said. I glanced back

down at the business card, and when I looked up, Ms. Davis was gone.

That was a very strange interaction. I guessed I was going to see this Molly Rose person after work.

And I had no idea why.

two

· · ·

lachlan

INDIANA UNIVERSITY BOASTED a sprawling campus with a winding creek and forested trails. I crossed over a bridge that led to gothic limestone buildings rising up nearly as high as the trees. After spotting Showalter Fountain—a sculptor's take on *The Birth of Venus*—in front of the auditorium, I noted the telltale signs of this campus's never-ending construction: traffic cones, caution tape and orange fencing. Fortunately, it wasn't blocking my path to the theater department.

I took the steps to the second floor two at a time on my hunt for room 204B, though I had no idea why I was in such a hurry. At the top of the stairs was a suite of offices with its main door open. A narrow hallway revealed six doors, A through F, so I headed to B. That door was also open.

I peeked inside and saw the occupant had her back to the door. Soft pink hair was piled loosely on top of her head in what I believed was termed a "messy bun."

Narrow shoulders filled out a short-sleeved black sweater, and a brightly patterned skirt flared out at her hips.

I knocked on the doorframe. "Uh…Ms. Rose?"

When she swiveled around to face me, I took in her exquisite pale skin, rosy cheeks, and round eyes. They were an unexpected shade of light green, framed by a pair of perfectly arched brows. "Yes?"

"I was told you needed help with something?" I waved her business card. "A Ms. Davis from the Biology Department gave me your card and asked me to meet with you this afternoon."

"Oh!" The single word came out as a chirp. Her eyes snapped to the embroidered name on my shirt. "You must be my Scotsman!" She rubbed her hands together as though she'd just received a birthday present. "Wow, Poe did not misrepresent you at all! Please, take a seat." She gestured toward one of the two chairs across from her desk.

I wasn't sure what to make of her statement. Maybe she needed some set work done? I didn't know why the theater department facilities folks couldn't do the work, but maybe my skillset was right for a particular issue she was having?

I folded my hands in my lap as she sat across from me, just smiling and staring. "So, what do you need?"

"Didn't Poe tell you?" She blinked in apparent confusion. "I need a Scottish actor for a play I'm producing."

What? I was damn sure this Poe person did not tell me that little tidbit.

"Actor?" I shook my head—now I was just as confused as she seemed to be. "I'm a maintenance guy, basically. Not an actor."

"But you *are* Scottish," she confirmed.

"I mean, yeah, I suppose I am, but I—"

"Well, will you at least audition for the role?" Her eyelashes fluttered, and the corners of her lips turned up as she stared at me with hope in her striking eyes. They were such an interesting color—so light, they almost didn't look real, and the way they contrasted with her pink hair was— "Lachlan?"

I snapped back to reality. "Please, call me Lan. Everyone does."

"Lachlan is such a…Gaelic name though." She stood up from her desk and smoothed down her skirt.

Now I got the full picture of her curvy figure. She was short—probably at least a foot shorter than me—with narrow shoulders, a rounded stomach and wide hips. Something about her curves woke up the sleeping dragon that was my cock.

I was around college-aged girls all day and nary a chubby. But this curvy pink-haired vixen was breathing life into me.

"So what do I need to do?" shot out of my mouth before I could tell her *no thank you, I'm not an actor. Good luck finding someone else.*

Her full lips spread into a smile that showed her front teeth. One had a little chip out of the bottom, and it was weirdly attractive. She reached into her desk drawer and pulled out a thick packet that was stapled in one corner. "This is the script. Hamish is the main character. You read his part, and I'll read Tony's part. That's his cellmate."

"Cellmate?" I looked down at the script. *What the fuck? Hamish is a convict?*

"Yeah, he's in prison," she explained. "He's a big, beefy Scottish guy with a thick accent and tattoos." Her eyes raked down my figure. "Do you have any?"

"Tattoos?"

Her eyes lit up. "Yes, do you?"

"Yeah, I got some."

She nearly squealed. "You do look the part for sure. I want to give it to you just based on that alone, but let's read these lines real quick. Your character's all brusque and tough, okay? Can you do that? With an accent?"

I barely suppressed an eye roll. "I guess so." Being a standoffish arsehole was definitely in my wheelhouse.

"Okay, here goes. I'll be Tony." She grabbed her own stapled packet and studied the page for a moment. Then she sucked in a lungful of air and blew it out.

The deep voice and thick New York accent that came out of her mouth shocked the hell out of me. "Ya think you can just get outta here, man? Where ya gonna go? Whudda ya gonna do?"

My jaw clenched as I read the line. "Dinnae matter, long as I'm no' here. I'd rather die than stay here."

"You prob'ly will, man," she said in Tony's voice. "They'll prob'ly shoot ya before you even make it over the fence."

"Am nae goin' over the fence, brother," I read the next line. "Am goin' under."

She shook her head, still in character. "Guess I'll see you in hell then, man."

My nostrils flared as I delivered the last line of the scene, "Aye, cannae be any worse than this place."

She put her script down on the desk and looked up, those green eyes stabbing right into me. "That wasn't bad. Your delivery is a bit stiff. We'd need to work on that."

"Would we, now?" I met her gaze, and as if they had a mind of their own, my lips began to curl into a smirk. *Where the hell did that come from?*

"Can you make a rehearsal tomorrow at four?" Hope beamed from those entrancing orbs.

It wasn't just my lips being controlled by some other entity—they'd taken over my tongue too. "Yeah, sure, that works for me."

She grinned and clasped her hands together as if it was the best news she'd heard all year. "Wonderful, thank you so much, Lachlan."

"Lan," I corrected her. Though, for that smile, I'd probably let her call me anything she wanted. I had no idea what I was getting myself into, but she made me want to get all the way in.

"I'll see you then." She was still grinning and rocking back and forth on her feet, which were clad in thick-heeled black combat-style boots, wildly contrasting with the full, feminine skirt. I liked her style. She was different.

As I turned to go, I heard her mutter under her breath, "I'm so glad my girlfriend found you!"

molly

"Well, do I know how to pick 'em or what?" Poe slung her arms around me and pulled me in for a kiss. "He's perfect, right?"

"Well, he's not an actor." I pulled back and continued into the kitchen so I could make myself a sandwich. Everyone else had eaten except for me—and apparently they neglected to leave me any leftovers. *Blurgh.*

"But he's still perfect for the part, isn't he?" Poe's thick eyebrows drew together as she surveyed me. "That accent, though...am I right?" She fanned herself dramatically—I was really starting to rub off on her, wasn't I?

"We'll have to work on his delivery," I noted. "And I

don't know how he'll respond to blocking, or if he'll have any problems memorizing lines, but I guess I don't have any other choices at the moment, and I'm running out of time."

"A thank you would be nice!" Pouting, she slid up next to me.

"Thank you, babe." I'd already changed my mind from sandwich to salad, so I was chopping lettuce and slicing a tomato. I set the knife down and turned to her. "How was your date last night?"

Cynda and Jason filtered in as if they'd heard my question and wanted a front-row seat for Poe's answer. "Hey, Molly," Jason greeted me, and Cynda wrapped her arms around me from behind and gave me an affectionate squeeze before they settled themselves in barstools at the countertop separating the kitchen from the living room.

"My date went really well," Poe reported. "I like her. She likes me. I'm sure we'll go out again."

"That's great, sweetie." I leaned down and pressed a kiss to her cheek. "I'm going to be so busy with this play for the next month. It's a great time for you to get to know someone."

Poe's eyebrows scrunched up as she stared at me. "That makes it sound like it wouldn't be okay if you weren't busy."

"I don't mean that at all," I clarified. "I'm totally fine with you having another partner. The timing is just convenient for me, that's all. Sorry I selfishly thought about myself in relation to your dating life." I rolled my eyes, then set down my knife and shook my head. "I'm clearly hangry. Sorry for all the snark."

"Hangry and stressed," Cynda added, patting my

back. "It's okay, Molly. We're all here for you. So, it went well with the Scottish guy?"

"Molly doesn't seem quite as excited about him as I thought she would," Poe complained. "Wait till you see him, Cynda. I'm pretty much totally gay, but he's quite the specimen of masculinity."

"Oh yeah?" Cynda's dark eyebrows arched. "Do tell!"

"He's brawny," I offered, sprinkling some shredded parmesan into my salad and adding a dollop of Caesar dressing.

"Tall, brawny, and has a Scottish accent," Poe enumerated Lachlan's finer qualities. "C'mon, Molls, you claim to be bi. Is he not your type?"

The truth was…if I had a type when it came to men, Lachlan would definitely be it. I didn't know what it was about tall, thick guys who looked like they could wrestle a bear, but I was down. And that was my first thought when I looked up from my desk and took in the imposing figure standing across from me.

As a matter of fact, when he offered to show me his tattoos, I might have swooned if I hadn't quickly tamped down my inappropriate thoughts about him and quickly shifted to Professional Molly Mode.

"Well, Molly?" Jason interjected. Now he seemed invested in this conversation too. "I know *I'm* not your type, so—"

When we first moved in with them, Jason tried to put the moves on me. He knew I was bi and wasn't dating any men, so he thought maybe I needed a penis in my life. Jason was cute, but the idea of dating a brother and sister was a little on the weird side, even for this diehard poly chick.

"I've been leading a perfectly happy penis-free life, you

know," I shared with the overly invested members of my polycule.

"Maybe it's time to get back on the horse, so to speak," Poe joked with me. When Jason started to snicker, the siblings lost themselves in a hearty chuckle.

"I don't see the humor in that." I took a bite of my salad and washed it down with a gulp of the leftover Moscato.

"Wait for her to finish eating," Cynda helpfully suggested. "Her humor sensors will hopefully reset when she's not hangry anymore."

They followed me to the kitchen table, where I sat down, then took another bite of salad. "Again, I'm sorry for my attitude, Poe. I do appreciate you convincing Lachlan to come audition for the part. I'm hoping it will work out."

They all took seats around me as I continued to devour my salad. "I'm sorry if I offended you with my horse comment." Poe reached out and took the hand that wasn't shoving salad into my mouth. "But you know I'm fine with you dating a man, right?"

"How did we go from casting Lachlan in my play to me riding a horse or dating a man?" Cynda was right; my sense of humor was returning now that my belly was getting full. "I mean, seriously, that's a big leap, even for you two!" I pointed my fork at Poe and Jason.

Jason shrugged. "Well, you haven't dated a man since we've all lived together—unless it was a secret fling. Did you have any secret flings?"

I batted my eyelashes and deadpanned, "Wouldn't be so secret if I told you, now would it?"

"But you *are* bi?" Jason pressed.

Cynda jumped to my defense. "A person's orientation

doesn't dictate who they date. A woman could be bisexual or pan even if she's only dated cis women. It's about attraction, not action. Though, judging by the way you drool over Henry Cavill…I think it's safe to say you're bi." She winked at me. She had a thing for him too.

"Thanks for that, Cynda." I swallowed down the rest of the wine. "She's right. I've always been attracted to men, but…well, to be honest, I've never had any luck in relationships with them."

"So when was the last time you dated a man?" Jason seemed to be awfully invested in this.

I hoped he wasn't interested because he was going to start flirting with me again. I truly wanted to believe he understood that ship had sailed. Without him.

"High school." I laid down my fork and blotted my mouth with my napkin.

"High school!" He sounded shocked. "That was ages ago!"

"Yes, I'm totally over the hill at twenty-eight. Geez!" I turned to my girlfriend, who was watching this conversation with interest. "Can I smack your brother?"

"If you don't, I very well might," she replied.

I folded my hands together on top of the table. "Settle in, my friends, for Story Time with Molly. You may want to grab some snacks."

Everyone cheered, clapping and getting comfortable, except for Poe, who declared that, in lieu of snacks, more wine was needed for story time. She opened a new bottle and grabbed three more glasses, and soon we were all ready to hear Molly spin a sad yarn of woe.

"Once upon a time, Teenage Molly was a little boy crazy," I began my story. I paused to take a small, delicate sip of the fresh glass of wine Poe had poured me. "Teenage

Molly was also chubby—not unlike Adult Molly, come to think of it. But Teenage Molly was much more self-conscious about her chubby self."

"I've seen pictures," Poe interjected. "Teenage Molly was totally adorable, as you can all well imagine, I'm sure." There were murmurs of agreement before I could go on with my story.

"Anyway," I waved my hand to the side to brush off their commentary, "there was this boy in my eighth-grade science class. He was my lab partner for dissecting a frog, and he asked me on a date. But then I found out he had just done it as a dare—his friends dared him to ask a fat girl out."

Poe smacked her hand across her face. "Assholes! What the fuck is wrong with people?"

I rolled my eyes. "Well, they were thirteen. Not that it's an excuse, but, listen, it gets better. If better actually means worse, you know?" I paused for their chuckles.

"So, my junior year, I went to prom with a fellow band geek named Alex Winston. It seemed to be going pretty well until we were on our way to the post-prom party, and he pulled over in this very rural area, like there were corn-fields all around and shit. In other words, it was any random back road in Indiana."

"Oh hell no!" Cynda gasped. "Sounds like something out of a horror movie."

"Just about," I confirmed. "Except, instead of stabbing me with a knife—or something even more gruesome—he proceeded to grope me and tell me he thought for sure I'd put out since I was fat."

"I'm starting to sense a theme here," Jason noted.

I smirked. "Then there was my senior year…"

"I'm afraid to ask." Cynda wrung her hands on top of the table.

"I was a theater geek, as you all know." There was a chorus of affirmatives and nods around the table. "So, our senior spring musical was *The Sound of Music*, and I played Maria."

"I can totally see that." Cynda grinned and held up her arms in a sweeping motion as she sang, "The hills are alive…"

"Anyway, the guy who played Captain von Trapp was named Eric Bartholemew. We'd known each other since third grade, and I'd always had a crush on him. He was smart—he was in the National Honor Society, so he was a nerd like me. But he also played basketball, and you all know how important that is in Indiana. Anyway, we had a backstage thing going during the entire show. We made out. He told me he really liked me, and all that."

"Aww, backstage romances are fun!" Poe chimed in. "So what happened with him?"

"What happened is, when the show was over, he wanted to sneak around like we did backstage instead of going out on dates in public. And then he asked another girl to our senior prom. I was heartbroken—absolutely devastated. My bestie confronted him in the cafeteria a few weeks after the show closed. He told her he liked me, but he couldn't date me 'for real' because," I gestured down my body, "you guessed it: I'm fat."

"Wow. Was The Asshole your high school mascot?!" Jason stood up, his chest heaving with a rage-y breath. He was genuinely mad on my behalf. He and Poe were originally from Connecticut, so maybe it was different there.

I shrugged. "I was bullied and teased from the time I was about nine until I went to college. College was a totally different experience for me. I met my first girl-friend, Jackie Stuchevsky, and she taught me so much about myself. In high school, I'd constantly been embarrassed and ashamed about my size. She showed me that size has nothing to do with beauty or sexiness."

"Damn straight!" Cynda said, then she burst out laughing. "Well, you know what I mean!"

"So you didn't date any guys after high school?" Jason questioned.

I shook my head. "I dated Jackie until she graduated, then we broke up because she went to Europe and never wanted to come home. She got a job over there and ended up getting married and having kids. We kept in touch for a while—we're still friends on Facebook." I smiled. "I think of her often. To say she changed my life is an understatement."

Everyone was quiet for a moment as I steeped in the memories of my first girlfriend with her long copper-colored hair and her piercing blue eyes. She had freckles and dimples and was just—God, I missed her sometimes.

"I dated a few other women in college, and then I had one serious relationship when I had my first job. I was a high school English teacher in Indianapolis before I started grad school, you know. I had a whole different life back then. You know I'm not out to my family, but, up in Indy, I could do what I wanted, and I didn't have to worry about my parents finding out down here in B-Town."

"But no men—not ever?" Jason seemed to be stuck on this concept. "Does that mean you're a virgin?"

"Excuse me?" Poe whipped around and smacked her brother on the arm. "How can she be a virgin when I fuck her silly almost every night?"

I burst out laughing. "Do you think lesbians are virgins because they've never had a dick in their pussy?"

Jason turned red with embarrassment. "Oh my god, you're right. I didn't even think about how stupid that sounds. What the fuck was I thinking?"

"Men think their dicks are so important, they can change a woman's identity," Cynda said with an eye roll. "Well, we all know that's not true. If dicks take your virginity, then maybe you're a virgin too, Jase."

Now he was laughing. "Who says I've never taken a dick?" He cocked his head and waggled his brows.

"What?!" Now Cynda was shocked. "You have?"

"I did some experimenting in college, like any good college student should." He batted his eyelashes with fake innocence. "And, honestly, I'd do it again—under the right circumstances."

Cynda pretended to be typing on her phone. "Oh, don't mind me, I'm just taking notes for future reference."

We all laughed before I chimed in again, "Well, I'm not a virgin to hetero sex either. Eric Bartholemew and I totally fucked backstage one night after rehearsal. Everyone had gone home, but we snuck into the dressing rooms. Later that night, we discovered we were locked inside the school, and the janitor had to let us out!"

"Oh my god!" Poe chuckled. "That's hilarious. You never told me that before."

I shrugged. "We also fucked a couple times after that— before the whole prom date incident. But that's the only dick I have to go by."

"Maybe you should try another?" Jason waggled his eyebrows at me. "One is a pretty small sample size."

"I think I'm good." I looked around the room at the smiling faces of my best friends. I was so lucky to have this group, where we could all be ourselves, and there was never any judgment—maybe some flirting or cajoling to try something new, but definitely no judgment.

I sighed and stretched my arms over my head. "Well, tomorrow is going to be a long day—our first rehearsal. Thanks for listening to me, guys."

"That's what we're here for," Cynda said, and Poe slung her arm over my shoulder.

three

· · ·

lachlan

LAST NIGHT, I lay in bed, tossing and turning. I couldn't get Molly Rose out of my mind. What was that last thing she said about her girlfriend? Did she mean like a girl she hangs out with—a friend who happens to be a girl? Or did she mean like a romantic partner girlfriend?

It was absolutely pointless for me to care about the answer to this vexing question. I wasn't looking for a relationship, anyway.

In lieu of chemical sleep aids, I opted to dig out the script she gave me earlier in the day. I figured it would put me right to sleep, just like Shakespeare always did.

Well, guess what?

I stayed up half the night reading the damn thing.

Which was why I was dragging my sorry knackered arse into this rehearsal with all the apprehension of a Scotsman wearing a kilt on a windy day. Molly's play was damn good. There was no way in hell I could do the role justice, but I wanted to try—for her.

By the end of practice, I was feeling defeated, and I had a killer headache to boot. I knew I'd have to memorize my lines, but I didn't realize there was a whole other beast called blocking. Unsurprisingly, as most of the cast began to file out of the black box theater, Molly called me over. I was about to get a scolding.

"Hey, Lachlan, can I talk to you for a minute?" She stood beside a bench, the script clutched in her hands, and her knuckles were white—that was how tightly she was holding it.

I nodded, feeling dejected. It was no surprise I was bad at this. Talk about a self-fulfilling prophecy. "Hey, I'm sorry. I've never done this before."

She laid a gentle hand on my arm and captured my gaze with her own. "Hey, it's okay. Listen, I really appreciate that you're doing this as a favor to me—you have no real reason to other than the kindness of your heart. Are you sure you want to do the show?"

"I was that bad, huh?" I collapsed onto the bench, the hard wood hitting my tailbone and sending a shooting pain down my leg. Just what I deserved.

"No, no," she said. "Not for a total newbie. Not at all." She shook her head emphatically like she felt it was her duty to convince me I didn't do a shite job of it.

She sat down next to me, leaned toward me and placed a hand on my leg. She probably didn't mean it as anything more than a comfort, an assurance, but heat shot up my thigh and pooled right between my legs. I shifted a bit, laying my script over my crotch so she wouldn't see the bulge forming there, but she moved her hand before anything too embarrassing could develop.

"Look, I respect your time," she said. "If you aren't able to put the effort in, I'd rather you tell me now than a week before we open, you know? I have a bunch of eager Acting 1 students who would love to cut their teeth on this role. Would they be as convincing as *you* could be, with some work? It's highly doubtful. But I need to know you're committed to working hard—because you'll need to. Not trying to be a jerk, truly. I just want to be straight with you."

Having grown up playing a ton of sports, including rugby and football, her words came across like a coach's. I had to respect it. She was saying I was in control. It was up to me.

For some reason, it made me want it that much more. Not to mention just being around her. Okay, so she was probably only into girls, but—there was something there pulling me toward her. I didn't quite understand it.

I wanted to know more. I needed to. This bonnie lass with the pink hair and combat boots impressed me. Being in her presence felt like standing in the sun. Normally a grumpy arse like me preferred the cold *dreich* days of my homeland to bright sunlight hitting my face. But I not only wanted to stand in her presence—I wanted to bask in it.

"Well, what do you say?" She stood up and folded her arms across her ample chest.

I rose from the bench and faced her, looking down into her beautiful face. Her pale skin shimmered under the harsh lighting, and her pink hair piled on top of her head practically glowed. Tonight she wore a skirt in a purple and gray camouflage print and a black V-neck sweater that accentuated her curves. Her clunky thick-soled black combat boots were paired with rainbow-striped socks. She was a mess—a gorgeous, sexy, sunshiny mess.

"I want to do it," I said firmly. No wavering in my voice. No hesitation in my answer.

She nodded. "I hoped you would." A tiny smile curled her full lips, but she quickly licked them, and her smile disappeared as she picked the script up again. "I think you will do better when you're off-book. You'll be able to emote more, which is what's really missing. You're reading the words right now, not feeling them."

She stepped closer to me, and the hair on the back of my neck stood on end. She reached out and placed her small hand on my chest, right over my left pec. "I need you to feel the words, Lachlan. Feel them here."

Her touch sent those electric shocks to my extremities again, and more blood pooled in my groin. I choked out, "But how? How do I do that?"

"Would you be willing to meet with me for some private acting lessons? We'll run lines, work on your blocking, and we'll get you caught up with the rest of the cast. They may be younger, but they've been doing shows since they were probably twelve, thirteen years old. Middle school drama club, high school musicals, community productions—you name it. You're starting from scratch."

She just asked me to meet with her in private? *Hmmm.* Before I could consider whether or not that was a wise idea, I blurted out, "Yeah, sure. Whatever you need."

Whatever you need?

Fuck. I might as well write her a blank check.

But I wanted to. I wanted to see those lips curl up in a smile for me...because of me.

"Can you start tomorrow after practice?" Her head

tilted down toward her phone as she studied the screen—looked like her calendar app.

"Uh…" I thought about the fact that it was six o'clock now, and we'd started practice at four o'clock. I came directly from work. I hadn't eaten dinner yet, and I was starving. "What about dinner?"

"Dinner…" One eyebrow arched.

"You know, the third meal of the day?" I tried to suppress a smile.

She patted the ball of fluffy pink hair on top of her head. "Right, dinner. Well…we can Door Dash something after practice maybe? So we don't lose any time?"

"Yeah, that works." I patted my stomach, and a short, staccato chuckle came out of my mouth. "Growing lad, *ye ken*?"

"Right." She smiled. "So I'll see you tomorrow?"

"Yes, ma'am." I nodded and headed toward the door. As much as I wanted to look back at her, I successfully restrained myself.

I completely blew it up there, but she was so kind and gracious. I thought for sure she was going to kick me to the curb. She wrote a brilliant play, and she seemed to be an amazing motivator as well. Not to mention the fact she was sexy as fuck with those curves and combat boots.

Fuck.

What the hell was happening to me?

molly

"Well, how did it go tonight?"

I only took one step into the foyer before the questions started up.

"I'll tell you in a few. My stomach is in charge for the

next twenty minutes, or until it's full—whichever comes first," I answered my girlfriend's inquiry.

I was starving—again—and at least this time someone had ordered pizza, so I grabbed a slice and joined the crew in the living room. I noticed a new face and glanced around at the members of my polycule to see if someone was going to introduce me.

"Oh," Cynda dabbed at her mouth with a napkin, "this is my new friend, Darth."

"Hi, Darth, I'm Molly." I took a giant bite of pizza and just barely had a chance to swallow it before I cracked the requisite *Star Wars* joke. "Does that mean you've come over to the dark side, Cynda?"

On cue, Darth emitted a deep, rumbling chuckle. "Never heard that one before." There was plenty of snark in his statement, and his laugh was a little on the dark side too. He stood up and leaned over Cynda to grab another slice of pizza.

"Geez, Darth, why not just use the Force?" I teased him.

He growled back, "You didn't tell me you lived with an amateur comedian, Cynda." He plopped back onto the sofa beside my dear friend and then attacked a slice of Meat Lover's.

Cynda laughed a sparkling, twinkling little giggle, the polar opposite of Darth's. "Oh, honey, Molly's had a rough day. She's working on her MFA thesis."

His glare stabbed into me, unimpressed as he chewed his bite of pizza.

I went over and sat on the arm of the wingback chair where Poe was perched. "Hey, beautiful." I pressed a kiss to her cheek. "Going out tonight?"

She stood up, grabbed my hand and led me into the

kitchen where we had a little privacy. "Yes, Delaney invited me to join her party for D 'n D at the game shop downtown. They're starting a new campaign tonight. Is that okay? It starts at eight."

"I thought you hated Dungeons & Dragons." I shrugged. She must have liked Delaney an awful lot to agree to play an entire campaign. I guessed that meant she was going to be gone for the next several Wednesday nights.

"Well, I hated Jason and his friends when they played it in the living room loudly all hours of the night when I was growing up," she explained. "I swear, I never thought they would shut up some nights! I don't care what you rolled, or if your whole party fell off a cliff, you know? Not when I'm trying to fucking sleep."

Polyamorous folx playing Dungeons & Dragons was such a cliché. But whatever.

I patted her shoulder gently. "Okay, I don't care if you play. I just thought you hated the game, that's all."

"Hate the playa, not the game," she quipped. She wrapped her arms around my waist and pulled me flush with her body. She smelled like citrus and vanilla—her favorite body wash and lotion. "So, how did Mr. Scotsman do tonight at rehearsal?"

I sighed. "Well…it wasn't a total disaster, but it wasn't great. Like an F1 tornado as opposed to an F5."

"Very colorful analogy," she said, laughing.

"More like a metaphor," I corrected her. *Hey, I used to be an English teacher.* "But he's going to stay after practice tomorrow so we can run lines. I think if I can get him off-book, it will make a huge difference."

Her hazel eyes widened. "Whoa, you're staying late after practice?"

"Um, yeah? Is that okay?" If she was asking for my permission to play D 'n D, maybe she expected me to ask permission for this, though seeing as producing this play was my job, it seemed like apples and oranges to me.

"You like him, don't you?" My girlfriend stood there gawking at me, mouth open wide and hands on her hips. "It's the accent, right? Or is it the muscles?"

I scoffed. "I have no idea what you're talking about. He's going to stay after practice so we can work on his acting, which he currently sucks at."

"Work on his acting, right." She actually laughed. "It's okay to like him, you know. I wouldn't mind."

"You know what I think?" I leaned toward her.

"What's that?"

"I think *you* like him," I theorized. "*You* like him, and you'd like to date him, but then you'd have to turn in your lesbian card."

A high-pitched squealing laugh erupted with so much force, her shoulders shook. "I do think he's attractive, and that accent is hot as hell, but I have never dated a man, and I certainly don't intend to start now."

"Mmm-kay," I shot back. "Whatever you say."

"Exactly, whatever you say." She laughed again and slipped a long black duster sweater over her t-shirt. "It's fine to want some cock, Molls."

I rolled my eyes. "Words of wisdom right there, folks." I chuckled a few times as she pulled me into her arms and pressed a kiss to my lips.

"See you later tonight," she murmured against my mouth.

I squeezed her ass before pulling away. "Have fun!"

Then she was out the door, and I was alone with my script, a highlighter, and a red pen. I was going to work on this blocking, and I was going to come up with some exercises to help Lachlan find his footing as an actor.

Sagan gave me a nasty side-eye as he jumped down from his perch on Poe's pillow.

Just as soon as I get some wine…

I'd drained two glasses of wine, and I was still stuck on Act I. The problem?

Every time I started to work through a scene, I envisioned Lachlan in the role and…

Well, I got distracted.

First, I thought about what he might look like without his shirt on. I was sure he had big, well-defined muscles. Was he ripped? Or did he have that sexy big-boy look with a little bit of a pudge that would make him oh-so-fun to cuddle with? Was his skin smooth and man-scaped, or did he have a thick, masculine mat of chest hair?

I hadn't seen a man naked since high school. And that dude was hardly a man—he wasn't even eighteen yet. He was a skinny, wiry, bony kid with gangly limbs and fumbling hands.

I had gotten a look at Lachlan's hands tonight. They were big and strong, with thick fingers and tan skin made up of what looked like millions of tiny freckles. They were the kind of hands that knew how to work hard and fix things.

Were they the kind of hands that knew how to wring pleasure out of a woman? Did they know when to be gentle and when to be rough? Did they know how to find that sensitive bundle of nerves deep inside?

And his lips. I had paid attention to the way they moved as he spoke his lines, as his Scottish accent rumbled out in his deep voice. His lips were wide and full, outlined by the scruff of a short reddish beard. I wondered how that scruff would feel scraping across my smooth skin, if his lips would move across my body the same way they spoke his lines.

What the hell was I doing?

I shouldn't be thinking about him that way. I should have been thinking about coaching him to enunciate more clearly—it was going to be hard enough for the audience to understand his accent. He needed to slow down. He also needed to project. We'd work on speaking from the diaphragm.

And we'd work on his blocking. Making his movements seem natural. Angles—never having your back to the stage, creating an angle instead. Making sure other actors in the scene could be seen and heard.

Then I started thinking about those angles, and how I'd visually explored his posterior when he was working through the first scene earlier tonight. The length of his legs, the thickness of his thighs. The curve of his ass and how it filled out his work pants.

Fuck.

There I go again.

I looked at the clock and saw it was only ten-thirty. I didn't expect Poe to be home for at least a half hour. Heat had worked its way throughout my body, igniting every nerve and making blood pool in my core. There was a heaviness there, an ache. There would be no sleep for me tonight without resolving that dissonance.

After setting the script next to my empty wine glass, I slid down flat on the mattress, my head slightly propped up on my pillows. I was wearing an old, oversized *Joseph and the Amazing Technicolor Dreamcoat* t-shirt I'd gotten during a production from my undergrad days. The black background and the rainbow were both faded, but the cotton was so soft. I hiked it up around my waist and let my fingers trail down the peaks and valleys of my torso, all the way to where it met my thighs.

My palm cupped my mound for a moment, feeling the heat thoughts of Lachlan generated as it seeped into my skin. Then my index finger parted the seam between my lips, instantly gathering moisture as it traveled to my clit.

I gasped when I realized how wet I was. I never got that wet without even being touched.

What if Poe was right? What if I was wildly attracted to this man but afraid to admit it?

I might not be able to admit it, but my body couldn't deny it.

I reached up and pinched one of my nipples between my fingers as I stroked my clit with my other hand. *Oh god*. It wouldn't take me long to come like this.

I imagined those strong hands and those full lips; a deep, rumbling brogue in my ear; and those thick limbs holding me in place as he had his way with me.

And I hung there, suspended on that line between ache and ecstasy, for only a moment before erupting in exquisite pleasure, a short trip to heaven in rhythmic waves and gasping breaths.

I didn't even stir when Poe joined me an hour later.

four

. . .

molly

"SO, I need you to cross to center stage for this monologue when you first start it. Do you see that light up there?" I pointed, and Lachlan nodded. "That's going to be your spotlight once the lighting designer works her magic. You're going to stand right underneath it by the second line. That's your mark."

"Okay." He looked around the stage, which wasn't a stage at all but a square space with a curtain on one side and blocks of bleachers on the other three. "So…you keep telling me where to stand on stage, but…isn't there going to be a set? What's going to be around me? It feels weird to just be standing here with nothing around. Won't there be something to look at besides me?"

I chuckled at his sudden self-consciousness as I stepped over from my spot on the sidelines. "No real set. For one thing, it's a black box theater, and sets are generally minimalistic. And, secondly, I'm paying for this production myself. Not only can I not afford to build anything, but I almost failed stagecraft when I was an undergrad."

"What? You almost failed stagecraft?" Lachlan chuckled. "What do you mean? Like hammering nails and screwing shit in and stuff?"

"Yeah, yeah," I waved my hand in the air, "so hilarious. Make fun of the girl who couldn't drive a nail straight to save her life. I did fine in the set design class. Building them? Not so much."

His thick brows drew together. "And that's an actual class? Like a college class? Part of your degree?"

"Yeah, of course it is. There's a lot more to theater than just acting, you know. There's all the tech stuff—and some of it is really complex and technical. Lighting, set design, sound engineering, directing, costuming, makeup. I'm a playwright and director, but I had to take classes in all that other stuff too for my undergrad degree. And some higher-level stuff for my masters."

"So there are people who just build theater sets? Like for a living?" He looked amazed by this fact when I nodded. "If you could design a set for this play, what would it look like?"

I looked down at the script. I hadn't given this any thought at all because it wasn't going to happen. "That's a damn good question. I'd probably have some sort of scaffolding. It would be symbolic, right? Hamish is trying to redeem himself. Higher levels could be a metaphor for goodness, and lower ones for evil, or for when he hits rock bottom."

"Maybe you need a pit for that," he joked. "He really fucks up at the end of the first act, doesn't he?"

I nodded. "He's desperate. He feels trapped, and he knows it's not safe to run anymore. So, in the second act, when Ruth tries to help him, he doesn't want to accept her offer, but he doesn't feel like he has a choice. Him struggling with what to do is what leads to this monologue at the end of the third scene, the one we're working on now. All of his decisions up to this point are bearing down on him like a ton of bricks. His fight or flight reflex has kicked in. We need you to convey that, make the audience feel it right here." I formed my hand into a fist and pressed it to my chest.

"Right here," he repeated, mirroring my gesture with his own hand pressed to his chest. "I don't know the lines one hundred percent yet, but can I just say what I remember and try to do it in character?"

"That's called ad-libbing," I explained, "and, yes, let's give it a shot. I'm going to go sit down and watch. Don't forget your volume. Don't go so low that the audience won't hear you, and give yourself plenty of room for building volume at the climax of the scene. It should be a gradual crescendo."

"Got it." He nodded and took a deep breath, his chest visibly rising.

I sat down and kept the script beside me, closed. I just wanted to watch him, not follow along. We didn't have the lighting rigs set up yet—some lighting design students were going to do that for me. Lachlan wasn't in a real spotlight, so a shadow silhouetted his form as he began Hamish's speech at the end of Act 1.

The words were not important. I was listening to the timbre of his voice, the way it rumbled low before rising like a falcon soaring toward the clouds. Gone were his stiff and self-conscious movements like when he started yesterday. The words were spilling out, coming naturally, and his body was moving, muscles flexing, jaw ticking, fists clenched as the anger bubbled and gurgled in his throat. Once that anger filtered up to his mouth, and the veins in his neck began to pop, gravel hit his voice, thickening it, making it rasp and growl over his words.

Goosebumps prickled my skin as I watched him lose himself in the role, all raw, primal male energy as he raged about his misfortune, his sins, his utter lack of worthiness. How the only chance he had at life was to continue to sin, to choose the low road—no one would allow him on the higher one. He'd been banned. Excommunicated. Exiled.

This was the vision I'd had for Hamish MacGregor.

Lachlan was embodying everything I hoped and dreamed for this character, and he was turning my insides to goo.

lachlan

When I finished my speech, my eyes were closed. I didn't remember closing them. My throat felt raw and strained, but I didn't remember screaming. My muscles felt like I'd just gotten back from the gym, but I was still on my mark. It was like I'd had an out-of-body experience.

I looked up and saw Molly sitting where I'd left her on the bench, tears streaming down her face. As soon as we made eye contact, she leapt up, shouting, "Yes! Yes! That was it! That was exactly it! You did it!"

A wave of exhilaration washed over me, so intense, my knees almost buckled. I rushed to her. She looked so beautiful with tears streaking down her blushing cheeks. "Are you okay? Why are you crying?"

"I'm a crier, sorry!" She shook her head, and tears flew off in every direction. She wiped her eyes with her thumbs, smudging her eyeliner just slightly to give her an edgy goth look. "I'm just so happy you're getting it!" The tears continued to roll down her cheeks as she opened her arms.

I stood there for a moment, taking in the sight of her. I was still getting my bearings after having such a strange experience, and now she was crying and spreading her arms like she wanted to embrace. "So it was good? That's what you want from me?"

"Yes!" she cried. "Now, are you gonna give me a hug or what? I'm a crier and a hugger."

I was not a hugger, but when my eyes swept down her curvy figure, I was overwhelmed with a need to know what she would feel like in my arms. I swept her up into my embrace, squeezing her to my chest.

Time came to a crushing halt.

My heart thundered against my ribcage as her arms squeezed around me. My grip tightened, and I drew in the soft floral scent that wafted up from her bright pink locks. What was this woman doing to me?

She was supposed to be the director. I was supposed to be the actor. Her, the teacher. Me, the student. But all I could think about was finding out what her lips would taste like.

Unable to contain that need any longer, I pulled back and drilled into her green gaze. One finger lifted her chin toward mine, slowly, giving her plenty of time to tear herself out of my embrace.

But she didn't. She yielded to me, her eyelids fluttering closed as my lips brushed along hers so gently, so tenderly.

Electric sparks radiated throughout my body, starting at my lips and cascading to every point from my head to my toes. Just as I attempted to part her mouth with my tongue, she broke away and staggered back, seeming unsteady on her feet.

Her face had gone ashen. She was shaking her head.

"Sorry, god, so sorry. *Ah dinnae ken* what came over me —" I stammered, my accent thickening as my palms rose and I backed away. Cool air rushed into the space between us.

"I'm the one who's sorry," she claimed, wiping away another tear. "I just got caught up in the moment. You're a fast learner. I wasn't expecting you to—to nail it so quickly. I—"

All I wanted to do was kiss her again, prove it wasn't about my acting at all. There was an undeniable energy between us, and when our bodies were melded together, it was combining, growing, expanding like a brightening star.

She was as radiant as the sun. I shouldn't have been surprised by her gravitational pull when I was just a fading moon.

"I should go," she said. "I know we were going to order dinner, but—" She shook her head again, a small smile turning her lips up. "I think you came a long way tonight. Maybe you don't need these sessions, after all. Uh…I think you have a lot of, um, raw, natural talent…"

She let her words trail off as she went around the black box space, picking up her belongings: the script, a purse, a jacket. "I'll see you next week? No practice tomorrow since it's Friday. Um, have a good weekend, Lachlan. Bye now!"

And before I could even get one more word out, Scottish slang or otherwise, she had vanished.

Thursday night after play practice, it was tempting to go out with the rugby lads and get hammered. But I didn't—I wasn't a young stud anymore. I was thirty years old, and I couldn't show up at work hungover.

But it was so tempting because it might be a good way to eradicate Ms. Molly Rose from my mind. What the hell had even happened at practice? I'd been reviewing that scene—both my monologue and what happened afterwards—in my mind on repeat, and I only ended up more confused. *Ma heid's mince* was what we'd say in the Motherland.

I needed to get my head on straight. Fortunately, I had a few days before I would see her again. From now on, I needed to keep my hands, lips, and any other wayward appendages to myself and far away from her luscious, curvy body.

Damn it, there I go thinking about her again.

Friday was the gateway to the weekend, and the weekends were for rugby. My rugby teammates were my family, at least on this continent. I just needed to get through the day at work—and my boss was gone to boot. It was going to be an easy day.

Until it wasn't.

First, there was a leak in the water feature in the new biology greenhouse project. I spent most of the morning trying to figure out how to fix it without tearing the whole goddamn thing open. I had a headache, and I'd left my lunch on the kitchen counter at home. *Fuck.*

So, I went over to the IMU—the student union building —to grab a bite, which I hated doing because that place was always infested with people. And I wasn't a fan of people.

I ordered a couple slices of pizza and a soda and went

over to an isolated table by the window overlooking Dunn Meadow. I just wanted a little bit of peace and quiet—a pipe dream on a campus with over thirty thousand students. But before I could even finish chewing my first bite, I heard the clink of a tray hitting the table across from me.

"Hey, what's up, remember me? I'm Poe, we met earlier this week?" The brunette pulled out a chair and seated herself across from me with absolutely zero care for whether or not she was welcomed.

My eyes lasered into hers, trying to send the message, "Go away!" but it didn't seem to work. I barely grunted, and she just went on talking like I wasn't giving her a death glare.

"How's the play going? Molly said she was nervous about pulling it off, and I gotta tell you that a lot is riding on this play for her. Do you understand the gravitas of the situation?"

Finally, she stopped talking. I took another bite, chewed, and stared back at her.

She blinked big eyes at me and crossed her arms over her chest. "Well, do you?"

I laid down the napkin I'd just used to blot the grease from my mouth. "Why are you bothering me? Did you follow me over here?"

"Follow you?" She had a sparkling laugh. "Like, did I stalk you over here from the bio building? Um, no. I just happened to be grabbing lunch as well, seeing as this is a public dining facility. And when I saw you sitting here, I thought it was a sign I should come over here and tell you that you better work hard for my girl."

"Your girl?" My eyes bounced between hers as I tried to get to the bottom of this. Molly had referred to Poe as her girlfriend the first time I met her, but after our kiss last night, I thought she meant in the *friend who is a girl* kind of way and not in the *doing the nasty* kind of way. Or maybe that was just wishful thinking.

"My girlfriend?" Poe's eyebrows arched.

"You guys are a couple," I stated rather than asked. So *that* question was answered.

"Well, yeah." Poe rolled her eyes. "She didn't tell you?"

"We didn't talk about our personal lives," I fired back.

We only sucked face, and then she ran away. *Fuck.*

Did I almost convert a lesbian?

This Poe person was still talking, much to my dismay. "She and I live together…along with the rest of our polycule."

"Your what now?" I blinked a few times, repeating that word in my head, but, no, that didn't make any more sense of it.

"Polycule," she said again. "A group of polyamorous people who are sort of like a family, interconnected in some way. Well, part of our polycule is my brother, so he and I actually *are* family, but—"

"You guys are polyamorous?" I had heard that term before, but it seemed like more of a mythical thing, like the Loch Ness Monster.

The woman cocked her head. "I guess she didn't tell you?"

"Why would she?"

Poe's cheeks flushed a little. "Well, I thought—"

"Thought what?"

"She was flustered when she came home last night from practice. She didn't want to talk about it, but the night before, I swear I heard her say your name in her sleep, and, well—" She stood up. "I shouldn't be here. I shouldn't be interfering in her love life—"

"Are you trying to hook me up with your girlfriend?" I narrowed my eyes. I couldn't make sense of this crazy conversation. Maybe I was the one having a dream?

"No, I just...well..." She took a deep breath and straightened her spine. "If you hurt my girlfriend or fuck up her play, there will be consequences."

I stifled a chuckle. "Oh, yeah? What kind of consequences?"

"My entire polycule will come after you," she threatened. "And my D 'n D party too."

I shook my head. Was this woman for real?

"Okay, have a great weekend!" she blurted out, and before I knew it, she was gone. I didn't even get a chance to ask her if she was really threatening to sic a bunch of role-playing nerds on me.

Then, when I returned to the biology building and checked my email, there was one from my boss's boss: the head of facility management for the entire campus. He wanted to see me in his office first thing Monday morning.

I slapped my hand against my forehead. *Fuck me sideways! Is it four o'clock yet?*

five

. . .

molly

WHEN I GOT HOME from campus, Poe was stretched out on the sofa with a washcloth over her head. "Are you okay? What's wrong?" I rushed over to her. Sagan saw me coming, immediately leapt down and scampered off down the hallway.

She took out her earbuds and tossed them on the coffee table. "I took the afternoon off," she said, sighing dramatically. "They were doing more work on that stupid fountain in the greenhouse, and it gave me a headache. Loud damn machines!"

"Didn't you say that's where Lachlan works?" I asked, and she immediately bolted up as though she'd been miraculously cured.

"So, speak of the devil, guess who I ran into today at lunch?" She threw the washcloth next to her.

"Uh, I'm gonna guess Lachlan." I crossed my arms over my chest. Why did talking about him make me so uncomfortable? *You're the one who brought him up, dumbass.*

"Yeah, he was over in the IMU noshing on some pizza, so I asked him how the play was going," she revealed. "He's a man of few words. Maybe he just used them all up in practice this week."

I flashed back to last night. He did use a lot of words. Well, he used his mouth a lot, anyway.

I hadn't been able to stop thinking about him since he kissed me.

"I'm really impressed with his progress," I stated neutrally.

Well, I thought it was neutral, but my girlfriend saw right through me. "Why don't you just admit you have the hots for him?"

"Have the hots for who?" came a sing-song chorus of voices as Cynda, Darth and Jason all frolicked down the hallway, presumably coming from the bedroom. From the flush on Cynda's cheeks and neck, I'd just about bet on it —and I highly doubted they'd been sleeping.

"I think we should be the ones interrogating you guys," Poe said, smirking. "Having fun back there? Fuck, glad I was wearing my earbuds."

"We were counting on it." Cynda smiled deviously. "And, let me guess, you guys are talking about Lachlan."

"Why does everyone think something is going on between us?" I protested, my eyes darting to each member of our polycule plus Darth, though it looked like he was already well on his way to becoming a full-fledged member.

"I heard you screamed his name in your sleep," Darth said with a shrug. "So, that may relate to your inquiry."

Ugh, have I mentioned how much this guy annoys me?

"Screamed his name in my sleep?" I whipped toward Poe. "Why didn't you tell me?"

She smiled sheepishly. "I didn't want to embarrass you, sweetheart. I may have let it slip during breakfast this morning after you'd already left for campus."

"Yes, this is *much* less embarrassing. Thank you for watching out for me." I punctuated my sarcastic apology with a big-ass eyeroll.

"Sit." Cynda gestured toward the cushion next to Poe.

"What is this, an intervention?" My brows furrowed as I scanned the small crowd again. They were all smiling, and not confrontationally. One thing I'd learned now that I lived in a loving, polyamorous household was that these folks almost always had my best interests at heart.

It was a lot different than growing up the daughter of a minister in a very conservative, traditional, religious household.

You heard that right. I'm a preacher's kid. It explains so much, doesn't it?

Growing up, a sit-down like this—being confronted by my parents or other family members—was what my mother called a "Come to Jesus Meeting." And it meant I was about to get lambasted for something I probably couldn't even control (examples: my weight, my smart mouth, my failing math grade, and/or some boy in youth group who couldn't keep his hands to himself—yet him groping me was somehow *my* fault because I had boobs and therefore tempted him.) Sometimes my infraction would simply be that I wasn't making my parents or other family members "look good."

Appearances were everything when I was growing up.

Is it any wonder I now have pink hair, tattoos, multiple piercings, and I'm "one of those theatre people"? Not to mention me being bisexual and polyamorous.

"It's not an intervention," Cynda said kindly, "but we all think it's curious how this Lachlan character has essentially dropped into your life—complete kismet, if you ask me—and you seem to like him and are attracted to him, but you're so adamantly denying it. We just want to know why, that's all. It's perfectly fine for you to have a crush. But why lie to us and yourself about it?"

The weight of the truth Cynda just dropped on me pressed against my chest, making it difficult to breathe. "You're right. I think he's hot as hell." I bent down, burying my face in my palms as I admitted in a mumbly garble, "And he kissed me last night."

At first, my admission was met with silence.

I thought they hadn't heard me.

And then…

"What?!" Poe leapt off the sofa and, after one giant bound, landed right in front of me. She dropped to her knees and lifted my chin with one finger to look at me. "He kissed you?"

I huffed out a sigh that lasted for like ten seconds straight, I swear.

"There are several reasons I'm resistant to this whole thing," I attempted an explanation. "Most of which, as you are well aware, are related to my experiences with boys in high sch—"

"I hardly think you can compare adolescent males with mature adult males," Darth interjected, like I gave a crap what he thought.

I ignored him, but, of course, Cynda had to be all gentle and sweet about it. "It's not fair to Lachlan to lump him in with some seventeen-year-old douchecanoe," she said. "So, what else ya got?"

"Well, I'm the director, and he's an actor," I said. "It's not professional to get involved with a member of my cast."

"Maybe not," Poe agreed, "but this play isn't going to last forever. It will be over in a month, and then you can date the whole cast if you want. I certainly don't mind." She waggled her brows.

I scrunched up my nose in disgust. "Eww. Most of the cast is like nineteen years old!"

"Right, but Lachlan isn't. He's gotta be, what, late twenties, early thirties? In other words: your age?" Poe guessed.

"I don't fucking know." Once again, my head went into my hands, where I pushed against my temples, trying to ease the headache forming there. Was Poe's headache contagious, or was all this talk about boys and kissing leading to its natural consequence?

Play with fire and expect to get burned. Right?

"I think I need to meet this guy," Cynda said, fanning herself. She was still flushed from her earlier activities.

"Look, nympho," I turned to her, "if anyone in this polycule is getting it on with Lachlan Adair, it's gonna be me. Got it?"

As soon as the words tumbled out, both my hands flew to my mouth in shock. I was just joking, but—sometimes truth is born out of humor.

"I think you just proved to yourself how you feel," Jason suggested. "Why not keep an open mind and see where things go?"

"I still want to meet him," Cynda insisted. "Invite him over for Sunday dinner? I'll cook. I just wanna hear that accent." She turned to her two lovers. "Naturally, you would both be the beneficiaries of any effect said accent has on me." She used air quotes for "effect."

I rolled my eyes. "I am not inviting him here. I barely even know him! He kissed me, but then I ran like a stupid idiot. I don't know if he will even want to mess with a drama queen like me. Ironic, I know." I stood up, more frustrated with myself than I'd been in a long time.

"I don't have time to deal with this right now." I sucked in a deep, fortifying breath. "I have to work on my blocking notes and practice agenda for next week, and then I have to mentally prepare myself to deal with my family tomorrow."

Poe grabbed my hand and squeezed. "What? You didn't mention anything about that."

"It's my sister Meredith's bridal shower," I sighed. "It's at the church. There will be approximately fifty extremely pious women from my parents' congregation reminding me that I'm the heathen sister. But Meredith would be upset if I wasn't there, so I'm gonna suck it up and go."

Poe's expression softened. "Do you want me to come with you?"

She asked, but she already knew my response. I slowly shook my head. Not one family member had a clue I was bisexual, that I lived in a polycule, or that I was romantically involved with a woman and had been for three years. They believed my roommates were necessary to help me with rent—well, that wasn't a lie. Being a grad student meant subsisting at near poverty level.

Finding out the truth would completely gut them.

lachlan

My entire body felt like one huge bruise after one hell of a rugby match. Good thing I was headed to the drink-up afterwards with my buddy Sam. I was going to need a shit ton of beer to numb the ache I felt in every limb.

"Whoa, that last try was incredible!" Sam praised as he cranked the wheel toward the tiny downtown pub where we always hosted the opposing team after a home game. "I can't believe you made it with five of their guys chasing you down."

"As soon as the ball hit my hands, I knew I could score," I reminisced. All the pain was worth it. We won thirty-five to twenty-nine, thanks to my try.

"And score you did!" Sam pulled into a tight parking space. His truck was so big, I seriously doubted my ability to open the door and get out. I was a big guy at just over six feet tall and 250 pounds.

"Uh, you may need to pull back and let me get out first. No way I'm clearing that." My thumb jerked toward the window to show the narrow space between vehicles.

"Not with that huge ego you're sportin' after that try!" Sam joked as he shifted into reverse and backed up several feet.

"Thanks, laddie. My ego and I owe ya one." I clapped him on the back before opening the door and swinging my legs out. When my foot hit the ground, a shock of pain raced from my knee down to my toes. *Damn it.*

I limped in beside Sam to cheers from our team. "There's our Man of the Match!" our coach shouted, gesturing for me to join him on the tiny stage set up in the corner of the pub. I didn't realize we'd arrived so late, but Sam had to run by his house to drop his girlfriend off.

She didn't think she could handle the gratuitous drinking and bawdy rugby songs while she was six months pregnant. I couldn't blame her. We did tend to get a little rowdy.

I stood beside the Man of the Match from the other team with huge steins of beer poised and ready to gulp. On a count of three, it was down the hatch as we raced to see who could finish first. I slammed my mug down on the counter in only a few seconds' time, while my opponent was sloshing beer out of his mouth and still had half a pint to go.

My coach grabbed my hand and threw it up in the air in victory. Everyone went wild! I shook hands with my opponent, his coach and captain of their team before heading over to where my own teammates had gathered in the three booths in the opposite corner.

"Lanny, my man! Lookin' good out there!" Burke, our Eight Man, pounded me on the back.

"Thanks, lad. You looked good out there too." I smiled at the server when she set another beer down in front of me with a wink. I'd had a brief fling with her last year, and it seemed like she wanted to give it another go.

Burke must've thought so too because he elbowed me in the ribs as soon as she left the table. "She's into you, man. Did you see that wink?"

"I'm not blind," I threw back, and everyone around the table chuckled. Last week, I might have flirted back and tried to see it to fruition, but this week…

This week was different. In the course of a few days, I'd been completely thrown for a loop by a beautiful pink-haired playwright. I hadn't been able to get her out of my mind—then I saw her girlfriend on campus yesterday, and now I didn't know what to think. She threatened me not to ruin her girlfriend's play. What did she mean by that? Ruin it how?

I wondered if Molly told Poe about our kiss.

"So, are you coming or what?" Burke slapped his hand down on mine to get my attention.

"*Och*! What the fuck is wrong with yeh, yeh bawbag?!" I demanded, rubbing my now smarting hand with my other one. Fuck! I couldn't handle any more pain today.

"I asked you three times if you're coming to my Halloween party. The fuck is your problem?" Burke fired back.

I looked around the table at my teammates' faces. They were all nodding along as if to prove Burke's point that he'd asked me three times. I thought I only lost a second thinking about Molly, but apparently it was longer.

"When and where?" I threw back the rest of my beer.

"It's at my farm just outside of town, last weekend of the month. You can bring in a date if you want. In fact, you should bring that hot waitress. What's her name? Stephanie?"

I had to delve into the recesses of my mind to pull out her name. "Yeah, that sounds right." I grinned and held up a finger to ask for another beer. I needed to stop thinking about Molly. Maybe flirting with Stephanie would help. "Yeah, maybe I will."

Why, then, was I wondering what costume Molly would wear if I took her to Burke's Halloween party?

molly

My headache that started on Friday when I got home from work never fully dissipated, and it only amplified once I arrived at Meredith's bridal shower. My little sister was positively glowing. Her glossy dark hair was woven in an intricate braid that wrapped around her head with little curls framing her sweet heart-shaped face. She was full of smiles with twinkling eyes as she greeted all her guests, suffered through the ridiculous bridal shower games, and opened her gifts.

Afterwards, she pulled me aside. "Thank you so much for coming, Sis." She wrapped me in her spindly arms. She'd gotten all the height and willowy-ness of my dad's side of the family. I'd been blessed with the short, curvy stature dictated by my mother's genes.

"Wouldn't miss it for the world," I assured her, forcing my smile a little wider than I felt.

"I know this isn't really your scene, Molly." She gave me a sympathetic look as she packed up some of the loot she'd scored in a big plastic tote. My parents were in the process of loading down their car with all the gifts while Meredith and I organized them.

"Well, to be honest, it wasn't so bad." I gave her a heartfelt smile of reassurance as I tucked cards inside an empty bag that featured a blushing bride holding a bouquet close to her face. The flowers of the bouquet were glittery and three-dimensional.

She took my hand into hers. "You're still sure you want to be my maid of honor? I don't want you to feel uncomfortable in church." She cleared her throat. "I know you don't like being in the building," she whispered it like it was a state secret or something.

"It's not the building. I just don't like judgy people, Mer, but it's your special day, and I want to be part of it in any capacity you'll have me." I sighed. I loved her, but my throbbing head was making it difficult to play the role of Devoted Big Sister at the moment.

"I hope you have a special day of your own someday, Molly." The expression on her face was bordering on pity. I knew my family thought I never dated anyone. Even though they'd met her in passing, they had absolutely no clue Poe was my girlfriend.

Much to Poe's dismay.

I felt bad about it too. But if I paraded her around my family, it was going to cause a lot of trouble, especially if my father's congregation found out his daughter was romantically involved with a woman. Not to mention the fact that the only way I could afford to go to graduate school was because of some money I'd inherited from my maternal grandfather. If my parents found out about my relationship, they'd surely figure out a way to deny me those funds, which were in a trust that they controlled. I was planning to use the rest to finance a move to New York when I was finished with my MFA. I knew starting off as a newbie playwright in NYC was going to be hard, but my inheritance would buy me some time to establish myself.

Poe and I had discussed it many times. She didn't want to be a secret forever, and I couldn't blame her. I'd met her family—they lived in Connecticut but had visited us in Indiana. She was looking forward to going out in public as a couple in the Big Apple, where we could be whoever we wanted to be.

Here in Bloomington, Indiana...it was a different story.

Well, Bloomington was actually a somewhat progressive and LGBT-friendly town, especially for the Midwest. But it was small. And when you were the daughter of a local pastor, it meant a lot of people knew you.

"Maybe I will." I mustered up another smile just as my

parents entered the church's fellowship hall, where the shower had been held.

"I think we got everything but those bags." My dad pointed to the small pile we'd left on an empty table. We'd cleared away everything else.

"Are you ready to go?" My mother directed her question to my sister. She still lived with them—there was no way they would have condoned her living with her fiancé before the wedding. They were traditional evangelical Christians—so premarital cohabitation was out of the question.

"Sure, just a sec. I was telling Molly goodbye."

"Yes, goodbye, dear." My mother walked over and put a stiff arm around my shoulder. "Don't be a stranger."

I nodded and bit my lip to avoid saying anything else. My father simply nodded at me, and he and my mother left without another word. To say our relationship was strained was putting it lightly.

"Hey, maybe you could bring a date to the wedding?" Molly's eyes sparkled as if the idea had suddenly occurred to her, and she found it brilliant.

"Um, yeah, maybe." I shrugged, though I had no intention of bringing a date. Poe wanted to come, but I was afraid of how my parents would react to that. Even if we were there strictly platonically, I feared my father's congregants would gossip about his daughter's plus-one being female.

The last thing I wanted to do was steal any of the spotlight from my sister on her day.

But as I headed out to my car, I got a clear vision of walking into Meredith's reception on the arm of a very handsome Scotsman, who, in my wild imagination, was wearing a kilt.

And then I felt guilty because it wasn't fair to Poe that my family was so judgmental and backwards. But they would probably be overjoyed to see me with Lachlan. That made me ache for my sweet girlfriend. And for me too.

I shouldn't have to hide who I am just to keep the peace in our family.

six

. . .

lachlan

THE ADMINISTRATIVE ASSISTANT—WHO wasn't Poe—smiled and ushered me inside the dean's office. I thought I was meeting with the Head of Facility Services, but it turned out, I was meeting with him, the Dean of the College of Arts and Sciences, and others. Now I was more nervous than ever before. I couldn't figure out why some academic would want to meet with me, especially not one of the top administrators on campus.

I walked into the dean's conference room and saw familiar faces around the table: the chair of the biology department, the assistant chair, and two professors. This was really weird. Why were all these people waiting for me to arrive?

"Have a seat, Mr. Adair," Dean Terry's gravelly voice came from the head of the table.

I took one of the empty seats on the end and willed my palms to stop sweating in case anyone wanted to shake hands with me. I hoped not, but it was better than the alternative that kept going through my mind: I was getting fired. They weren't happy with the greenhouse project, and I was to blame. I designed it, engineered it and oversaw the entire thing.

"Lachlan, thank you for agreeing to meet with us today," Dr. Hammer, the head of the biology department, said. She cleared her throat and looked around the table as if she needed permission to continue.

"Uh…thank you for having me," I replied, forcing the pitch of my voice down at the end so it didn't sound like a question.

"I'm sure you're wondering why you're here," Dr. McCall, one of the professors I knew from the committee that helped design the greenhouse project, finally started getting down to brass tacks. He was a balding middle-aged man with ruddy skin, sharp blue eyes and wire-rimmed glasses.

Everyone gave a stiff chuckle as their gazes zeroed in on me.

"Yes, I'm rather clueless about the reason," I agreed.

"I'm Dr. Veda Indari," the other professor introduced herself. She had thick, black hair coiled into a large knot on top of her head, held by a tortoiseshell clip. "Dr. McCall and I are planning a semester abroad with students to do some research on Highland cattle."

Just the mention of something so synonymous with my homeland sent a thrill through my system. I didn't say anything, though, just waited for her to continue.

"We understand you hail from Scotland," Dr. Hammer filled in.

"I do," I confirmed, but I still had no clue what this had to do with me. I thought Highland coos were adorable—as did anyone in possession of a soul—but I didn't see what that had to do with my work as a facilities maintenance engineer.

"We'll be taking some equipment with us to aid in our research," Dr. Indari explained. "And we'll need someone who is able to help us assemble it, clean it, and fix it if anything should break. It's likely we will need some highly specialized custom-made apparatuses while we are there as well."

"Okay?"

This was where my boss took up the mantle. "Becky, ahem, I mean Dr. Hammer, and Dr. Terry asked if I knew of any employees who would be a good fit to go abroad for the semester and fill this role, and, naturally, I thought of you. Not only are you Scottish, so you'd be familiar with the culture and environment, but you're one of the most talented guys we've got." He pulled no punches. "The design work and implementation of the greenhouse enhancements were absolutely brilliant—I doubt an engineer could have done a better job with the design, especially since you were trying to incorporate the entire committee's ideas and were limited in terms of space and budget."

"Well, I'm flattered you'd think of me," I finally spoke.

"We wouldn't be leaving until February first," Dr. McCall announced. "But we need an answer from you by November first, so we can make other arrangements if you're not able to join us. You're absolutely our first choice to be on our team, though."

I wanted to ask *where do I sign up?* But something held me back. It wouldn't interfere with rugby—spring season wasn't nearly as important as fall. It wouldn't interfere with the play—it would be over by the end of the month. I couldn't really think of any drawbacks.

But I still wasn't ready to commit.

"I can absolutely let you know by November first," I said. "It's an honor to even be considered."

The professors went on to provide more details about the equipment and its specs, as well as the premise of the research they'd be doing in conjunction with scientists from St. Andrews University. But I tuned out after a while.

I was still trying to wrap my head around this incredible opportunity and why I wasn't jumping up and down to accept it.

I spotted Molly talking to a few of my castmates when I entered the black box theater. She had her back turned to me, and her pink hair was down for a change—it was longer than I realized, covering her shoulders with a little bit of a wave and flip on the ends. She wore a form-fitting purple sweater that hugged her curves and a pair of black leggings with white cats on them. On her feet, the ubiquitous combat boots.

She turned to me and gave a little tsk. "Nice of you to join us, Mr. Adair." She rolled her eyes and pointed at the clock. It was ten minutes past four, so, yes, I was a wee bit late. But I'd gotten called into my boss's office to further discuss my potential trip to Scotland next semester. He was happy for me, but clearly not thrilled at the prospect of losing me for a few months.

"We're blocking Act II tonight," she said. "I know we don't have Act I completely down yet, but I want to get Act II blocked so we can do a whole run-through for time.

It can't be over two hours, so I may need to trim a couple of scenes if it is."

The thought of memorizing lines that might later get cut didn't sit well with me, but what could I do? I'd spent yesterday nursing my rugby-related hangover and memorizing lines. My roommate made fun of me the entire time, but I got him to run lines with me so I could practice. I felt like I was getting the hang of this. It helped that my character was a dark, troubled soul who ended up becoming a badass—a badass who gets the girl in the end. Not too shabby, if you ask me.

We made it through the second act, but I was struggling. My mind kept wandering—it weaved back and forth between thinking about Molly and that kiss and contemplating the prospect of returning home, even if temporarily.

"Lachlan, your line," Molly called from her bench. She was clutching a script decorated in various shades of highlighter: pink, yellow, and blue. The pink almost matched her hair.

"Oh, sorry." I cleared my throat and looked down at my own script. I realized I'd missed my entrance and lost my place entirely. *Fuck.*

"Kady, go back to your monologue in front of the judge," Molly instructed the woman playing opposite me.

The blonde rolled her eyes before she faced the pretend bench where Dalton, playing the judge in my case, presided over the pretend courtroom. "The defendant is clearly innocent of murder, as it has been proven he was framed." She hit the next mark in her blocking as she crossed the stage.

"Was Mr. MacGregor an honorable man who was simply at the wrong place at the wrong time? No, he was involved in some questionable activities, to be sure. But I can personally vouch for the defendant's redemption," she said. "I've seen it with my own eyes, and I believe with my whole heart he's ready to walk the straight and narrow."

"Judge Hall," I added, standing from my mark, which was supposed to be the witness stand, "what can I do to prove I'm a new man? Ask me any question, and I'll show you my truth. I'm under oath."

"Lachlan, you're going to have to emote a bit more there. Otherwise, it just sounds flat and almost sarcastic," she coached me.

I nodded.

"Go back. Do that line again," she directed.

I repeated the line, trying to get my posture, tone, and facial expressions to all convey the sincerity I knew my character needed to express in this moment. But about midway through delivering the line, I realized that, if I went to Scotland on this special assignment, there would be no Molly there.

What?

Why would that matter?

Then I was irritated with myself for even making that connection because it made no sense to me. It shouldn't be a factor in my decision at all.

Yes, I'd kissed her, and, yes, we were doing this play together. But, after this play, we were both going back to our own lives. *And, for fuck's sake, she has a girlfriend!*

"Lachlan," she practically growled my name. Before I could answer, I noticed she was scrubbing her hands down her face in frustration.

"I'm sorry." I shook my head and sucked in a deep, cleansing breath. "I'm having a hard time today."

She glanced down at her phone, obviously checking

the time. It was only five, but she looked like she was done for the day. "Alright, everyone, today was clearly a waste of time, so thanks for that."

She pursed her lips and looked at her cast. "Sorry, I—I just thought we'd accomplish more, that's all. But it's Monday, and you're all volunteers, and I really should just be grateful you're here. I know you're all working hard, and I appreciate you. I'm going to give you the rest of the night off so you can maybe work on your lines, get some rest, and I'll see you tomorrow at four. We'll try Act II blocking again, picking up in Scene 2. Does that work for everyone?"

There were murmurs and nods all around. I headed over to grab my backpack—I'd changed out of my uniform shirt and into a Metallica concert tee before practice. I was planning to talk to Molly before I left, but she was chatting with Kady. I honestly didn't want to make her any angrier than she already was, so I tried to slip by without her noticing.

But just as I got to the door, she barked, "Lachlan, don't leave. I need to talk to you."

molly

This man is going to be the death of me, isn't he?

He froze in his tracks after attempting to slip by me without me noticing. After asking him to stay behind, I held up a finger to let him know I needed a moment to finish speaking with his castmates. I wrapped up my conversation with Kady and turned to Dalton, who was next in line. But as I was talking to him, my eyes were drawn to Lachlan's broad chest and muscular arms. He really filled out that t-shirt, which was tight across his pecs and biceps. I never knew Metallica could look so sexy—it wasn't exactly my genre of music, but it did look good on him.

A fleeting image of him in that t-shirt plus a kilt flashed into my mind. *Oh, fuck.* Why did I keep imagining him in a kilt? What the fuck was wrong with me?

Dalton seemed to be satisfied with the answer I gave him, which, honestly, I had no clue what I'd even said, but the sophomore grabbed his backpack and rushed off with two other male cast members, saying something about pizza and Monday night football.

I glanced around the theater and realized Lachlan and I were alone.

"You wanted to see me?" He turned stormy-gray eyes on me, looking all innocent, like he didn't just wreck our second-act run-through.

"Yeah, um, what the hell happened to your face, first of all?" I gestured to his left eye, which had a ring of purplish-blue around it.

"Rugby," he answered simply, then shrugged.

Great. Now I was picturing him running around a rugby field with a bunch of other hot guys. *Not helping.* "And is rugby something that's going to be happening through the rest of our production?"

"Aye. I'm not giving rugby up, sorry." He shifted his feet apart, taking a broad stance that conveyed a bit of defiance.

"I'm not asking you to," I snapped. "Just wondering if you're going to have a black eye during the performances?"

"They can put makeup on it?" He gave another shrug.

"Why were you so distracted today?"

To be honest, I was afraid of his answer. It probably

had to do with what happened the last time we saw each other.

You know, when his lips accidentally crashed into mine, and I didn't stop him from making a long, thorough, spine-tingling apology—with his tongue.

"Look..." I closed my eyes for a moment and tried to reset myself back to Professional Molly Mode. "I know you don't have to do this show. I know it's asking a lot because you're not a student, and you're not really going to get anything out of this other than good karma for doing a poor grad student a favor, but—"

"I want to do it." He looked into my eyes, and his expression softened. "I'm enjoying it, to be honest. I just had a weird day, and my head's not in the best place. Then there's what happened last practice—"

"Right," I agreed, "which I was hoping we could put behind us and move on—"

"Why don't you let me take you to dinner?" he offered, the barest hint of a smile lifting the corners of his lips. "Mother Bear's?"

I should have said no. I thought we'd agreed to order something in and have a working dinner on the nights we ran lines together. But the director in me had already written tonight off—as far as it being productive was concerned. Maybe getting to know my cast member better would help me help him? In a strictly professional way, of course.

"Okay," I agreed. "Mother Bear's. Are you parked around here?"

"At the biology building," he said. "I'll meet you there in, what, fifteen minutes?"

I nodded. I wasn't going to say it was a date, because it

wasn't. I firmly stopped those words from slipping out of my mouth.

On my way to my car, I texted Poe.

Molly: Hey, going to grab pizza with Lachlan and talk about his acting, or lack thereof.

Poe: Don't be too hard on the lad. Find out if he owns a kilt. Cynda wants to know.

Molly: Fuck you guys. I'll be home later.

Poe: Take your sweet time, love. I might see what Delaney is up to tonight.

Molly: Enjoy!

seven

. . .

molly

"HOW DID you end up in the U.S. anyway?" So much for talking about the play.

Lachlan set his current slice of pizza—he had already devoured two others—back on his plate and wiped his hands on a napkin. "I was an exchange student fail," he admitted.

"What do you mean?" I popped the last bite of my breadstick in my mouth and waited for him to explain.

"I came over at age seventeen for an exchange student program, and I never wanted to leave. I mean, I had to go home briefly here and there, but I came back on a student visa and went to college. Then I got a work visa. And I just haven't been particularly motivated to go home."

"Really?" I blinked.

He leaned forward and settled his gray gaze on me. "Aye, lassie, I may look like a daft overgrown oaf, but I'm the proud owner of two bachelor degrees, one in philosophy and one in art."

"Philosophy? Art?" I shook my head. I would have never guessed. "Wow, you're kinda blowing my mind right now."

He crossed his thick arms over his chest and smirked. "Which part, the degrees, or what they're in?"

I nodded. "Both. Did you go to school here?"

"Aye, so when I came as an exchange student, I stayed with a nice family in Fishers, up by Ind—"

"North side of Indy," I finished for him. "Don't forget, I'm a townie."

He chuckled and dabbed at his face with a napkin. "Right. So you said your dad is a minister at a local church. What denomination?"

Talking about my family made me uncomfortable, but I wanted to be as open as he was being. "Oh, it's an independent church—non-denominational. Super evangelical. Super conservative."

"Gotcha. Wow."

I shrugged. "I guess we both have surprising backgrounds, huh?"

"I don't know—I'm not too surprised. Don't preachers' kids have a bit of a reputation?" His eyes twinkled as they raked down my face to my chest.

I tried to steer the conversation back toward him. "So then what? You ended up working in maintenance?"

"Well, not a lot of jobs for folks with bachelor's degrees in art and philosophy," he admitted. "Not that I didn't try. I wanted to stay in Bloomington—I love it here."

"Nice. So I guess you're sticking around for a while?" I didn't know why, but I felt a sense of relief that he wasn't going to be heading back to his homeland anytime soon. Silly, really, since I was planning to move to New York.

"Well…about that…" His voice trailed off, and he took a sip of his beer.

"Oh, so you *are* leaving, then?" That relief I'd felt was instantly crushed, and my lungs squeezed hard. Again, for no apparent reason.

"No, no," he shook his head, "not leaving permanently. It's just, the reason I was so distracted today was because I got an offer to travel to Scotland this spring semester with a group going over from the biology department to do some research on Highland cattle."

"Oh." I looked down at my hands. Why did my heart drop when he said that? "The whole semester? That's exciting. What would you be doing?"

"I guess maintenance guy stuff." He shrugged. "They were happy with my recent work on the enhancements to the biology building's greenhouse. I'm really just a glorified handyman though."

"Glorified?" My eyebrows waggled. I was trying to be facetious, but I didn't think he took it that way because his lips pursed, and his eyebrows drew together.

"It's not exactly what I want to do with my life," he said. "But it's steady, and I can stay in the States, at least for now. I don't know if it's a great idea for me to go back home anyway."

"Whoa, so much to unpack there." I smiled, realizing the conversation had taken a much more serious turn than I anticipated. "So…what did you want to do with your life?"

He looked up at the ceiling for a moment as if he needed to collect his thoughts. Then he brought his big, meaty hands to the surface of the table and threaded his thick fingers together. He was being very careful about how he responded to my question, and that intrigued me.

"I wanted to be an architect or an engineer," he said. "But I didn't do well enough in math for either one. So much math." He shook his head. "I've always had a talent for building stuff. I can design it, and I can build it. When I'm doing the design work, it doesn't feel like math. And it sure as hell isn't calculus or linear algebra."

I snickered. "I'm not a math person either." I shook my head, the giggles starting to erupt. "I mean, obviously. I'm a playwright. I fell in love with the theater at age seven when I did my first show, and I've written my whole life. It seemed completely natural to bring my two loves together. I guess that explains why I'm poly—"

I froze right then.

I took a quick drink of my soda, which burned down my throat. I started to say something else, but when I looked up, Lachlan was staring at me with a quizzical look.

"Poly?" He blinked a few times.

"Um, polyamorous," I explained. "Sorry, it's probably TMI. I just don't have a good track record of keeping TMI to myself."

"TMI?" he repeated. "Why do I feel like you're speaking a different language than me all the sudden? And not because you're American and I'm from the U.K."

I laughed again and tried to choose my words as carefully as he just did. I wanted to back up and ask him why he didn't want to return permanently to Scotland, but I knew I'd opened a can of worms, and now I'd have to address said worms.

"TMI means Too Much Information," I explained. "I'm just an open person. I tend to overshare. I was trying to make a connection about me combining my two passions —theater and writing—and my being polyamorous, or being bisexual, for that matter." I gasped, shocked I'd let even more TMI slip, and my hands flew to my mouth. "What's in this soda? Truth serum?"

He cracked an adorable smile and scratched at the stubble growing on his chin. "So how does this relate to Poe—the one who got me into this whole mess? And accosted me the other day at the IMU, I should add."

"Yeah, sorry about that." I shrugged. She was assertive, what could I say? "Yes, she's my girlfriend," I shared. "But we have an open relationship. We're free to explore relationships with other people."

"Is she bi as well?"

I shook my head. "No, she only likes women."

"But you like men as well." His gaze stabbed into mine.

It was a good thing I hadn't just taken another drink, because I very well may have spit it all over him. Shit, I did not expect our conversation to go anywhere near here. I expected to talk about him, not me. And it was my own dumbass fault for mentioning I was poly and bi.

Unless there was a part of me that wanted him to know…you know, so informed decisions could be made.

"I do," was all I managed to choke out in answer to his question about liking men. I was about to tell him that it had been years—a whole decade—since I'd dated a man, but I, for once, decided to keep my tongue in my mouth and not provide unnecessary details.

I also realized just then that his "But you like men as well" was actually a statement.

Not a question.

Like he knew the territory we'd just crossed into involved a big, thick wall of tension springing up between us. We were sitting here all platonic-like, talking about ourselves. And then, all the sudden, we were forced to face this spark between us.

Because it was there. Clearly.

Having not been interested in dating men for over a decade, I'd turned off my flirting sensors where males were concerned. I was surprised I could even recognize there was something brewing here, but I wasn't completely clueless.

I mean, him kissing me was a pretty big fucking clue.

"I'm glad to hear that," was his response, and that pretty much sealed the deal because the look in his eyes was hungry.

And not for pizza.

Which we'd pretty much already demolished at this point.

"Hey, do you need to be getting home?" He looked down at his phone for a moment and then back at me.

"Yeah, probably. But Poe is out tonight so…no hurry." Well, my holding back info didn't last long, did it?

"Where are you parked? I can walk you to your car."

Campus was well-lit, and there'd still be plenty of people out at this hour, so I wasn't too worried about walking alone, but it was very gentlemanly of him to ask. "I'm parked in the library lot today."

"Okay. I'm actually just down a block here off Third Street. Do you mind if we walk to my truck, then I'll drive you to your car?"

"Oh, yeah, I guess that makes sense." I reached for the bill, but he jerked it out of my hands.

He shook his head. "Allow me."

"You're doing me such a huge favor by being part of the show. It's the least I can do," I insisted.

He only glared at me, resolute.

"We can split it?" I suggested.

"*Och*, Molly. Just say 'thank you' and leave it at that, lassie." He rolled his eyes as he put cash in the tray. "Let's roll."

He waited for me to stand up, and then we walked out of Mother Bear's together. Fall was settling in, and a crisp breeze whipped through my hair, blowing it right in my face. I wished I'd brought a heavier jacket, but it was my bad for being a lifelong Hoosier, yet still not able to predict it would be raging hot during the day and frigid at night. *Duh.*

"I'm just over here." Lachlan gestured toward one of the staff lots at the edge of campus. I wasn't surprised to see he drove a truck, one that would take a little effort to climb into with my five-feet-nothing frame.

"Do ya need hoisted up?" he teased me.

"You just wanna touch my ass," I joked back. There I went again. Blatantly flirting.

He turned the key in the ignition and revved the engine a bit. "Well, I'm not gonna deny that."

A thrill raced through me, making me shiver. And not because of the cold. "I think I can manage."

He turned out of the lot and headed down the street formerly known as Jordan Avenue—I was having a hard time remembering to call it its new name—until he came to the library parking lot. "Which one is yours?"

"Last row there closest to the theater." I pointed to the left. "It's that yellow Volkswagen Beetle."

"Wow, are you serious right now?" He shook his head, obviously trying to figure out a good way to razz me about my ride, but he was apparently unable to come up with something clever.

"Well, I've got pink hair, and I'm a polyamorous

bisexual playwright. What the fuck do you expect?" I turned toward him and was surprised to see he'd already shifted toward me, his gaze locked on me as he leaned forward into my side of the cab.

But he didn't say a word. He just stroked his rough fingers down the side of my face and let out an audible wince.

"What was that for?" It came out in a choked whisper.

He sighed. "Your cheek is so soft, and I already know your lips are too. And all I have been able to think about for the last four days is kissing you again."

I didn't miss a beat. "So what's stopping you?"

"The fact that you're essentially my boss—at least when I'm on stage. The randomness of us meeting…" His voice trailed off. "Not knowing if you were into men."

"Well, we cleared that last one up."

Did I really say that?

I couldn't deny it any longer. I wanted his lips on mine again too.

And, like him, it was all I'd been thinking about for four days.

I closed my eyes as he leaned even closer, his head tilting as his lips blazed a trail through No Man's Land until they staked their claim on mine. I didn't know why it felt appropriate to make a war reference here, but it did. I had been battling this attraction since the first time we met, and I was waving the white flag of surrender.

"Fuck," he breathed out against my lips, making them quiver as his tongue brushed the seam. Desire flooded every pore in my body as I opened my mouth to accept his advance—his army crushing mine in defeat as I succumbed to his hands threading through my hair and him pulling me onto his lap.

Straddling him wasn't easy—my legs were short, and his whole frame was so broad—but I did my best. Arms wrapped around his neck as he grazed his way down my neck to my breasts. His hands cupped them, squeezing almost too roughly, and I realized in that moment I wasn't dealing with a high school boy. I'd never been touched by a real man before, and I was used to Poe's soft, gentle touch.

Lachlan wasn't Poe. That was for damn sure.

Especially because I could feel the bulge of his manhood pressing against me as he pushed me down and ground up into me. "Fuck, Molly, you make me want to do things to you—things we might both regret."

"I don't do regret," I fired back. "It's much like TMI. I don't believe in either of them."

"Don't say that, or I'll put this truck in drive, take you to my place, and fuck your brains out."

"Is that a threat or a promise?"

eight

. . .

lachlan

EVERY SINGLE LIGHT through town was green. If that wasn't an omen, I didn't know what was. Molly had fallen silent after our kiss, and we might have both been in a state of shock that this was even happening. Weren't we supposed to be talking about the play?

I turned off the highway, onto the road where my roommate and I shared a house. I really hoped he wasn't underfoot. He could be quite aggravating, but at least he always paid his rent on time.

I pulled into the driveway and parked on my side of the garage. My roommate's car wasn't there, and that was when I knew God was definitely on my side. The roommate had just started dating someone new and was spending a lot of time at her place. The stars were somehow aligning, almost like the Man Upstairs knew how badly I needed to get laid.

The last woman I dated was a biology professor, and she was certifiably insane. She wanted me to move in with her and knock her up. After I put a ring on it. That was after a month of dating! She once pulled me into a maintenance supply closet in the bio building and fucked my brains out. Yeah, the sex was out of this world, but even the best pussy isn't worth that amount of crazy.

Molly didn't strike me as crazy. She was eccentric, of course. She was a writer and actor, and those types were always the best kind of freaks. I hoped that translated to the bedroom.

"So, this is my place," I said in Mr. Obvious fashion as I turned off the truck's engine.

"Shall we?" She was nearly breathless as she turned to me, the light in the garage creating a gleam in her eyes.

She didn't have to say another word. I hopped out of the truck and went around to her side to open her door and help her down since it was a pretty big dismount for someone of her stature. She grinned, nodding in thanks before she followed me to the door. As soon as my hand touched the handle, the barking commenced.

I sighed, and Molly immediately gushed, "You have a dog?"

"I do." I opened the door, and my Scottish terrier bounded into my arms like her legs were made of springs. *"Aye, hullo, Miss Bonnie Skye, hoo's it gaun? Did yeh get yeh some scran yet?"*

I looked over at her bowl, and it was empty, which meant she'd either scarfed down every morsel of her dinner, or my roommate had forgotten to feed her. It was probably the former, but I poured some kibble in her bowl anyway while she sniffed out our visitor. She was a spoiled little lass, no doubt about it.

"Hope you don't mind dogs," I said as my girl got a little overly familiar with Molly.

She bent down and gave Bonnie's shiny black coat a few affectionate strokes. "No, I love them! Always had them growing up, but Poe is a cat person, so that's what we have at my house. Her cat, Sagan, hates me, though."

"Oh, Bonnie loves cats—loves tormenting them anyway." I shook my head. "My roommate had a cat for a bit, but it hated the dog, and all it did was hiss and bat at her, so he ended up giving it to his sister."

"Gotcha." She smiled and shifted her weight from one foot to the other.

"Do you want something to drink?" I refilled Bonnie's water bowl, then opened the fridge door to see what we had in the way of human libations.

"Water is fine," she said, but her attention was on her phone. "Sorry," she glanced up quickly, "I need to text Poe and let her know where I am."

I set two water bottles on the counter. "Will it be a problem?"

"Oh, no. She's practically been begging me to fuck you!" She giggled as she slid the phone back into her purse.

"Begging?" I blinked a few times. "Gotta say, I've never encountered this situation before."

"Is it too weird?" She uncapped the water bottle and took a sip. "I mean, it's normal for us, so sometimes I forget it might be weird for other people."

Her phone chimed, and she picked it up to take a peek at an incoming text. She cracked up and held the phone out to me. Poe had sent her three emojis: tongue-out, thumbs-up, and an eggplant.

"Wow, I guess that means you have her blessing?" I wasn't used to my hook-ups needing to get an okay from their girlfriends, but it was kind of hot, to be honest. I took the other water bottle for myself as Molly laughed and nodded.

Bonnie Skye led the way, prancing down the hall to my bedroom. As soon as we crossed the threshold, she took a running leap onto the bed, springing off the cedar chest against the footboard and sticking a perfect landing. Her little ears perked up, and her eyes seemed to say, "It's bedtime, Daddy!"

Molly set her water bottle down on one of the nightstands. "She sleeps with you?"

I liked the fact that she just followed me in here as we casually conversed about my dog. There was nothing awkward about it. No pretense. We both knew why she was here, and I didn't need to jump through a bunch of hoops to make it happen. That must be another advantage of hooking up with someone who was polyamorous. I wondered how often she did this.

"Yeah, I mean, who could resist that face?!" I reached down and cradled her sweet furry head in my hands.

Molly grinned. "She is pretty adorable, but, to be honest, I'm not sure I'm comfortable having her on the bed while we fuck."

Most women would have used a euphemism there or would have trailed off without saying the word, but not Molly. She was blunt and direct. Another absolute turn-on.

I scooped Bonnie off the bed and took her out to the living room where her wee cozy bed was perched next to the sofa. *"Yeh stay here noo, mah wee bairn, an' Daddy'll come get yeh later."*

She looked a little confused, her head tilting as if to say, "But bed is in there, Daddy!" So I patted her gently and assured her I wouldn't forget about her. Hopefully she wouldn't cry and interrupt the evening.

I returned to my bedroom to find Molly had already stripped off her combat boots and her leggings, and was just about to lift her sweater over her head. I rushed to her side, wanting to be part of the action. "Whoa, hold on there, lassie. Why don't you let me do that?"

"Sorry, I just assumed you'd want to get the show on the road, so to speak." She let out a nervous laugh.

I stared at her for a moment, assessing. That was when I noticed her fingers were trembling. "Molly, are you absolutely sure you want to do this? No pressure at all." I raised my hands, palms out, toward her.

She looked down at the floor and shook her head. Then a grin broke out on her face as she lifted her eyes to me again. "Nothing's wrong. I'm just ready to go. Where do you want me?"

She posed in her lacy black bra and panties, her rounded tummy and thick thighs looking so soft and smooth in the dim lighting. Her breasts more than filled out the satin-lined cups, spilling over the top in the most delectable way. A soft flush had pinkened her cheeks and the top of her chest, and her pink locks brushed against her shoulders, emphasizing their roundness.

"Good lord, Molly, you're absolutely beautiful." I took a step closer to her, close enough to breathe in her heady scent—soft florals and arousal. "I'm not in a rush, and I hope you aren't either. It's been a while since I've had a chance to worship a goddess."

A nervous laugh spilled out. "I'm not in a hurry, but I thought—"

"Thought what? I would just *wham-bam-thank you-ma'am*?" My index finger brushed a tendril of hair away from her neck, leaving a bare space where I could paint a few gentle kisses.

"Well…" Her eyes closed when I reached behind her to unclasp her bra. "I didn't know what to expect exactly."

I groaned when her heavy mounds fell away from the bra cups and bounced against her ribcage. Fuck. I needed to spend some time getting to know those beauties. I reached out to trace the edge of her breast where it met her torso. She quivered under my touch, her eyes closing. I stepped back and watched her for a moment. She was trembling.

I pulled her down to sit on the mattress, then sat beside her. Her eyes popped open, and trepidation flashed across her face. I took her hand in mine. "For someone in an open relationship, it doesn't seem like you do this much. You seem really nervous."

She sighed. "I'm trying to pretend I do this all the time." She laughed a little, shaking her head. "I'm not a very good actress after all, am I? Guess I should stick to writing scripts."

I took her chin in my hand and gently turned her to look at me. "There's no reason to act with me. No reason at all."

She bit her bottom lip and blurted out, "I haven't been with a man in over ten years."

I swallowed down my shock at her statement. "Just women?"

She nodded. "But I'm bi. I mean, I am attracted to men —attracted to you—"

"That doesn't mean we have to—"

She reached over and squeezed my thigh just above my knee, sending a jolt of desire right to my cock. "But I want to. I want…" She buried her face in her hands and laughed again. I could tell she was the type of person who laughed when they were nervous. "I feel so—I'm not uncomfortable; that's not the right word. I just feel —vulnerable."

"Vulnerable," I repeated.

She nodded and stood up to face me. She was so short, she was now only a few inches taller than I was sitting down. I could very easily bury my face in her boobs from this angle. And, fuck, that was tempting.

She pursed her lips and cocked her hip, resting her fist on it as her eyes bounced between mine. "Look, I don't know why I'm telling you this. I didn't expect you to care that I was nervous, or I thought you wouldn't notice. I thought you'd just take me, and we could get this over with—"

I couldn't stop a frustrating grunt from rumbling up my throat. "You thought I'd just take you? Like…a horny asshole who doesn't care about your pleasure?"

She laughed. "Um, yeah—because that's what I was used to from men."

I pulled her into my arms. "Well, lass, I'm not a horny asshole who doesn't care about your pleasure, but if you want me to just take you, I am certainly up to the task. It's taking every bit of restraint I have not to completely ravish you. But I would never do anything without your consent."

Her eyes widened as she caught my innuendo. Then she bit her bottom lip and said, "Show me."

molly

Did I just encourage Lachlan to ravish me? To have his way with me?

The gleam in his eyes as he stripped off his shirt and revealed his expansive chest covered in a thick mat of hair told me, yes, I sure as fuck did. He had big, round, firm pecs and the kind of arms that could protect you from any number of dire circumstances, like an alien attack or the zombie apocalypse. His giant chest was heaving with his breath, and I was quite certain he would have been a gladiator in a former life.

"On the bed," he commanded, piercing me with those stormy eyes.

I didn't say a word, just backed toward the bed, never breaking eye contact with him, until my butt hit the mattress and I fell backward with the faith of a student doing trust exercises with a partner on the first day of Acting I. He was crawling toward me, a feral growl on his lips, within seconds. The deep sound vibrated in his throat, making my pulse race and my lungs squeeze in my chest.

He straddled me, lowering his heavy body on top of mine and caging me in—it should have felt restrictive but instead made me want more of him. My wish was fulfilled when his lips claimed mine, not in the gentle, tentative way they had explored when we were in the black box theater, but with the ferocity of a lion attacking its prey. Just when I thought my heart might explode, he broke away to trail down my body, licking, sucking, biting, teasing and torturing every single nerve along the path to my pussy.

None of the assholes I dated in high school ever went down on me. Only women had done that—and I couldn't imagine any man being as good at oral as a lesbian. But then Lachlan reached the apex of my thighs, and what he orchestrated there was nothing short of magical. The expert way he teased me with his hot breath, his humming growl and barely-there licks had me begging for more.

"Fuck, Lachlan," I ground out between sharp breaths, "what are you doing to me?"

"Showing you how a proper gentleman pleasures a lady," he answered with absolutely no hesitation whatsoever.

As I arched into him, he finally bestowed a tiny bit of mercy upon me. His mouth made direct contact with my clit as he slid a finger inside me and stroked my G-spot, and he had zero issues locating that baby.

I was rendered speechless, every muscle in my body clenching with a need for release, including those in my throat. I writhed against him, angling for more, harder, deeper, but he was going to make me work for it, revving up the pressure and speed incrementally before bringing it back down again. He was building layer upon layer of agonizing desperation in my core, so expertly crafted that the sensation extended to the whole of my body. I was floating in an ocean of aching and longing.

Then. He. Stopped.

I didn't know this man was a sadist, but—

Well, actions speak louder than words, am I right?

"Would you like to come, Molly?"

I resorted to grunting rather than verbalizing my utter desperation.

"You have to tell me, lass."

"Fuck, Lachlan…yes…please…" I forced the words out in a heaving rasp.

"*Och*, I like the way that last word sounds on your tongue. I almost feel like I'm directing you for a change, instead of the other way around." While he said this, he circled my clit with a finger of one hand while he slowly thrust into me with two fingers of his other hand.

Just enough to maintain my current level of arousal,

but not enough to sweep me over the edge, despite my hips driving up to meet the bristles on his chin, which felt pretty damn amazing.

"Please let me come?" It came out a whimper.

"What a good girl…" A wicked smile curved his lips before he lowered them again to my mound. He made a big, dramatic show of swiping his tongue over my engorged clit, making my entire body convulse. I was seconds away from detonation, and he was the one who lit the fuse.

Returning his dedication to the task at hand, he ramped up the thrusts as his tongue swirled in an intricate rhythmic pattern against my clit. When he sucked it into his mouth for a nibble, I exploded. All that tension he'd carefully mounted within me was sprung, shooting me to the stars and back as my body was racked with exquisite pleasure.

He lifted his hungry eyes to me when I finally came to and grinned. His face glistened with the aftermath of my orgasm.

"It's your turn," I choked out, trying to sit back.

He pushed me back down—not hard, but firmly, and shook his head. "Naw, if I need to let this aching, dripping cock settle down on its own just to prove not all men are selfish bastards in the bedroom, then I'm willing to do it, lass. *I dinnae need a single thing from yeh except to see that blissful smile on yer bonnie face.*" I loved the way his Scottish accent flared up when he wasn't trying to suppress it.

"Oh, Lachlan…but I want to." I slid out from under him as my energy returned full-force. "Did you say something about dripping? I think I need to see said cock, you know, for quality control purposes. To make sure it's as described—no false advertising, and so forth."

He chuckled, a deep raspy laugh that reverberated through my cheek as he wrapped his massive arm around me and snuggled me into his side. *"Och, I suppose it cannae hurt to show yeh the goods."*

I gasped when he unfastened his jeans and a mammoth cock sprang out.

I was not prepared for that.

I didn't know if it was because I hadn't seen one in person since I was seventeen, and the owner was my age, or what. But, holy fuck, I didn't know they came in that size.

Poe and I used vibrators sometimes, but usually small ones. She wasn't into penetration like I was, and she mostly used her fingers on me, and her tongue, of course. Was I even built for taking something that size?

"Well, did I scare yeh off, lass?" He looked down at me, but my eyes were still glued to his enormous erection, which was waving in the air like a proud flag on a breezy day.

"Um, not exactly," I choked out.

"Not exactly?" he repeated and laughed, a deep, sharp staccato beat.

He reached down and squeezed it from base to tip—hard from the looks of it—and a clear bead of fluid pooled on the slit before sliding down his shaft.

"As advertised," I helpfully pointed out.

"Don't feel like you need to do anything about it. It will go away eventually." He said it neutrally. I really tried to hear a tinge of self-pity in his tone. But it wasn't there.

"So, I could just keep staring at it, and not touching it, and eventually it will go away?" I questioned. Having not had access to one of these for a long while, I wasn't overly familiar with the specs.

"Um, no, lass, not as long as you're in my arms like this, and I can smell your sweetness and feel your soft skin next to me. No, it's not going to go away while you're right here," he admitted.

"Then how will it? *I* have to go away?"

"As soon as you do, I'll put my hand back on it like this…" He groaned as his fingers wrapped around his shaft again in a firm grip.

"Yes?" My interest was certainly piqued.

"Then I'll close my eyes and imagine you spread out before me, your beautiful curves on full display—a veritable feast."

"Oh, yeah?"

He closed his eyes now as if to demonstrate.

"And then what?"

"And then I'll stroke it up and down," he demonstrated as he spoke, "thinking about pumping into yer tight, wet pussy. I'll imagine your walls are squeezin' me, milkin' me, an' that yer so full of me, all yeh can do is moan and cry out my name as yeh come hard around me."

"Fuck," I breathed out.

"Do yeh want me to show yeh how I can come just thinkin' about yeh?" he rasped.

As much as I wanted to see the show, I also wanted to know what he felt like inside me. I wanted him to have the real thing, not just the fantasy. I wanted us *both* to have the real thing.

I slid from his embrace and lay on the mattress beside him. Then I tugged at his arm. When his eyes opened, he turned to meet my gaze.

I pointed to my pussy. "Show me here."

As soon as he began to climb on top of me, the sounds

of ear-piercing barking filled the air, and the garage door made a grinding noise as it opened.

"Fuck," Lachlan grunted, climbing back off me again. He looked down at his cock. "Okay, that sound will also make it go away."

"Damn it." I pouted as he moved off the bed and pulled his jeans back on, then I followed his lead, sliding my clothes back on as well.

"Guess you'll get to meet my roommate," Lachlan mumbled as he pulled his shirt over his head.

I fastened my bra. "Okay, give me a sec."

"Bathroom's through there if you need it." He pointed to a door I thought might be a closet, but apparently it was the bathroom. "I'll meet you in the living room?"

I nodded. "Thanks."

I finished getting dressed, disappointed we weren't able to level up after the epic oral, but my body was still tingling from the masterpiece that was his tongue. I was sure Poe was expecting me home anyway, so it was probably a good time to call it a night. I grabbed my phone and realized, with alarm, it was just after midnight. And my car was still in the library parking lot.

Shit! I certainly hadn't intended to stay this late.

I hightailed it to the living room, where Lachlan was holding Bonnie in his arms and talking to his roommate.

"Oh, hey, Molly," came a familiar voice.

My eyes widened as I took in the full view of his roommate standing there holding a bottle of water in one hand and a banana in the other.

"Oh, hey, Darth." I did a double-take. "Darth?"

nine

. . .

molly

"WELL?" Poe met me at the door, all wide eyes and smiles as I headed inside, shaking off the autumn chill.

"You're not going to believe this," I rushed out, still trying to get over the shock I received right before leaving Lachlan's house.

"What?" Poe stopped me from heading into the kitchen, where all I wanted was a bottle of water. I was parched. "He's got no skills? His house is infested with rats? His sheets were stained with unidentifiable liquids, but it sure looked like blood?"

"What the fuck? Where are you getting any of that?" I studied my girlfriend's face. Was she hoping things went badly?

"You're as white as a ghost," she explained. "I mean, even paler than your normal pasty-pale skin tone, Molls. What the hell happened over there?"

"I did see a ghost, I suppose." I laughed, thinking about it. "Darth."

She blinked three times in rapid succession. "What do you mean, Darth?"

"Like Darth, Cynda's new squeeze? He's Lachlan's roommate."

She visibly shivered, like her cat Sagan did when he was kicked off the sofa. "Wow, really? From what I know about both of them, I can't envision that arrangement working out."

"Yeah, it's definitely a shocker." Having satisfied at least a portion of her curiosity, I went after that much-needed drink. But when I pulled open the refrigerator door, there were no water bottles to be found. "Fuck! Am I the only one around here who can put water bottles in the fucking fridge?"

It never failed. They could take the bottles *out* of the fridge, but no one seemed to know how to put new ones back *in* the fridge. Supremely irritating.

"There are some in the pantry," Poe pointed out.

"Yeah, room temperature ones. All a girl wants is a cold drink, for fuck's sake." I was irritable. Especially since I still hadn't figured out why Darth hung out with our polycule, listening to us blabber on about Lachlan, and never once piped up to say, "Hey, that's my roomie you're talking about."

"Sorry?" My girlfriend shrugged, a sheepish smile plastered on her face. "So, what happened with Lachlan? I can't believe all you're talking about is Darth. Don't you have anything to report in the *hot dude in a kilt* department?"

"He wasn't wearing a kilt," I assured her as I begrudgingly took a bottle from the stash in the pantry. Then I loaded up my arms and carried as many bottles as I could handle to the fridge, carefully arranging them on one shelf.

I had a feeling those would be all gone by the next time I wanted one.

"Oh, well, that's a shame. But hopefully that means he wasn't wearing *anything*." She gave me a dopey grin.

"How could Darth not put two and two together that we were talking about Lachlan, and he lives with Lachlan? We said his name several times. He knows about the play, and Lachlan even said he helped him run lines."

She shrugged again. "I don't know. He seems to be a bit of an odd duck. Maybe he just didn't want to share. Maybe he was trying to be discreet?"

I rolled my eyes. "Well, Mr. Dark Side of the Force interrupted what was turning out to be a pretty enjoyable evening."

Poe rubbed her hands together. "Now you're talking. What happened?"

I decided not to hold her in suspense any longer, but I did have a moment of panic. I hadn't really dated anyone else since I started seeing her. She was the one who had other partners. I had been too busy with school. What if she wasn't really okay with me seeing other people?

"Stop holding out on me, Molls," she demanded, tapping her foot on the floor impatiently.

"Well...we fooled around," I blurted out. "He went down on me—"

"Nice! Was he any good?" She licked her lips suggestively then performed a little dance with her tongue.

"Um...yes, actually." Just thinking about his mouth on me sent a shudder through my core.

She laughed. "You sound surprised!"

"Well, I'm used to women, and everyone I've been with —including you, my love—is magically skilled. So my expectations are high. I really didn't know if he'd meet them."

"But he did?" she clarified, eyebrows arched.

Guess I'm really going to tell her everything, huh? "Oh, yes!"

"So then, what…you returned the favor?" Poe seemed to be just fine with the information, even happy for me.

"Well, I was going to… Got to the point of the big reveal, and then Darth showed up, and Lachlan's dog went nutso barking."

"Oh, he has a dog. You'll need to wash your clothes. Don't bring them into the bedroom. Sagan won't be happy." She held up a finger and wagged it at me. Then her eyes narrowed. "Wait, what do you mean by the big reveal?"

"I mean I got to see his cock, Poe," I stated matter-of-factly.

"Oh, right." She said it like it was the most boring detail in the history of details. Complete disinterest.

I couldn't help but laugh, but when I thought back to the mental image I'd snapped of it, I was impressed all over again.

"Must've been noteworthy, judging by that dreamy look on your face," she teased me.

"It was…well, it definitely wasn't like ones I have been intimate with in the past," was all I could say.

She swatted at me. "So, you're saying he's hung."

I bit my lip, trying to suppress a grin. "I'm no expert, but it seemed he was packing some heat."

"Well, good for you." She yawned. "Delaney and I did the deed tonight too."

"You did?" I leaned in. I'd been waiting to hear about this for a while. "I thought you said she liked to wait?"

"Well, I guess I convinced her otherwise." Poe pretended to brush an imaginary piece of lint off her shoulder. "Not a bad night's work."

"What do you mean?" I drained the rest of my water bottle.

"Well, I think I made her come like eight times. And she's a squirter."

"I know how much you love that." I liked seeing Poe so cocky and proud of her handiwork. And tonguework.

She was beaming. "Yeah, she made a huge mess. Had to wash her sheets and all that. The whole nine yards."

I grinned. "Sounds like we both had a successful night, then?"

"I think we did." She wrapped her arm around me. "Now, what do you say we hit the hay?"

"Did you get an orgasm tonight, babe?" I asked as we walked down the hall toward our bedroom.

"No, tonight was about Delaney…"

"Well, then, I think you deserve a nice big O before we go to sleep."

This play was…coming together.

I could hardly believe it. We had two more weeks until opening, and I might just pass my thesis and be the proud recipient of a master of fine arts this December. It was pure exhilaration to think my hard work might actually pay off —and soon.

Not to mention the fact that Lachlan was coming into his own on stage. His scene work with Kady tonight was incredible. And I planned to tell him so.

My undergraduate cast members all scattered after I announced we were done for the night. But one big burly body remained. My sexy Scotsman.

"Hey, so I hope things weren't too awkward tonight," he said, approaching me. The scruff on his face had grown out enough that it now qualified as a beard. He still wore his uniform pants, but he'd changed into a t-shirt with a flannel shirt over it.

I faced him, trying to suppress the grin that seized my mouth every time I saw him now. "Define awkward."

He looked around as if trying to make sure we were truly alone, then he stroked a thick finger down my cheek and bit his lower lip while he sucked in a deep breath, like he was trying to take in my essence. "Awkward like, every time I see you, I just want to strip you down and plant kisses all over you."

"Um, well, in that case, it was just the right amount of awkward," I assured him, smiling.

"The other night was…" He shook his head. *"Och, ah dinnae like that bawbag roommate of mine comin' home when he did, but—"*

I had no idea what he meant by *bawbag*, but I got the impression it was an insult. "So, you had fun?"

"I think that's safe to say. Every time I think on it, this happens." Before I could ask him what he meant, he took my hand and placed it right on his crotch, where his bulging erection rendered any need for clarification completely unnecessary.

"I like that you're so forward." It was refreshing to deal with a non-poly person who didn't want to play games. That had not been my experience before, but then again, I'd always dated women.

"So, you had fun?" he repeated my earlier question.

I rocked back and forth in my boots. "Oh, yes. Five out of five stars. Would fool around with you again."

"A glowing review." He pursed his lips like he was trying to keep from smiling.

"So, what's on the agenda tonight?" I gathered up my notes and highlighters and stuffed them in my bag.

"I'm at your disposal, Madam Director." He gave a deep bow, and when he rose, a grin was splitting his face.

A thrill raced through me as I admitted something I didn't expect to reveal: "I kind of liked it when you were in charge," I decided to throw in some Scottish slang of my own, "*ye ken*?"

His eyes glimmered with lust as they raked up and down my body. "Is that so?"

I nodded, hoping that knowledge, plus a nod to his native tongue, turned him on as much as it did me.

"Is there any reason we can't visit your office to run some lines?" He put the last few words in air quotes.

"I believe that is exactly what my office was intended for." Biting my lip to suppress my grin, I led him to the staircase outside the black box theater. In moments, I was unlocking my office door, and he was pushing it closed behind me.

As soon as the lock clicked into place, my heart began to thunder in my chest, wondering what he was going to do next. He looked around the office, assessing, before plopping down in my chair and rolling it back from my desk. His finger pointed to the furry rug under it. "On yer knees, lass."

A wild jolt danced up my spine as I found myself responding to his command with zero hesitation. I looked up at him, awaiting further instructions. My mouth began to water when his hands went to his waist, unfastening his belt and work pants.

His chest heaved as he surveyed my eager face, a storm brewing in his eyes. The thick accent he poured on in his role as Hamish MacGregor was still in effect as he admitted, *"Ye ken how hard I came thinkin' boot yer mouth on my cock after yeh left the other night?"*

I shook my head. No words managed to squeak out.

"Not as hard as I'm gonna come in yer pretty mouth right now." With that, he reached inside his pants and pulled out his beautiful, thick, intimidating cock.

My lungs squeezed at the sight of it, veins bulging and the tip glistening with a pearly drop of his essence. I had never sucked a cock before.

Never.

I was afraid of choking to death on that thing, but I pulled up my proverbial big girl panties, scooted between his massive thighs, and looked up at him with willingness in my eyes. Yes, there was the slightest bit of panic, of fear there too, but it seemed to only make him harder.

"God, Molly," he breathed out, his voice little more than a deep rumble, his accent thickening, *"what the fuck are ya doin' tae me?"* He reached down to thread his fingers through my hair, pulling my mouth to his manhood.

My tongue darted out, tentatively at first, swiping up his shaft until the liquid pearl melted on my taste buds. It was salty and slippery and immediately made me crave more. I'd never tasted it before—I had no idea what to expect.

My lips wrapped around his head, and I drew on the extensive knowledge I'd gleaned from watching porn—mostly gay porn, if I was honest—and I sucked him as deep into my throat as I could and held him there.

He gasped and moaned as saliva filled my mouth, and I sputtered as he pushed me a little farther than my comfort zone. Then he released me, and I drew in a breath before my mouth moved back up the length of him, feeling the smooth, slick skin of his shaft glide against my lips.

I swirled my tongue around his head, and his whole body jerked at the sensation. *Oh, so he likes that.* I made another pass, performing the same maneuver but a little faster this time, a little harder.

"Fuck, Molly, how are yeh so good at that?"

I wanted to tell him probably from watching gay porn, but my mouth was full. I established a steady rhythm, moving up and down his cock as the muscles in his thighs tensed. One of my hands got in on the action, stroking in unison with my mouth. He guided my other hand to his balls.

"Touch them," he instructed, "not too hard."

I complied, adding that to my repertoire as the sounds that came out of his mouth were generated deeper and deeper in his throat—incomprehensible, primal sounds —*also coulda been Gaelic, for all I know.* Couldn't understand a fucking word of it, but I knew in that moment I wanted to make him come. I wanted to know my mouth had coaxed the cum out of his balls, shooting deep down my throat.

ten

. . .

lachlan

ALL COHERENT THOUGHT had vanished from my head. It was only my cock and Molly's mouth on it—those were the only two real things in the universe as every drop of available blood in my body surged south, making my cock ache in its painfully engorged state.

"Fuck, Molly, yer gonna make me cum, woman. Are yeh ready fer this?" I didn't know if I could hold back this tsunami for a second longer.

She wanted me to be in charge and direct the action—a reversal of our regular roles. My director's notes were as follows: *be a good girl and swallow every drop of the load I'm about to shoot down your throat.*

Her response was garbled when I took her face into my palms and pumped into her mouth, my hips thrusting like they were hydraulic. Her face was turning red, saliva dripping out around me as I edged closer to losing control.

"Fuuuuuuck!" I grunted as my balls tightened and cum rocketed out. She choked, sputtering as I held her mouth steady, not ready for her to let go. "Every drop, lass. Swallow every. Last. Drop."

When I opened my eyes again, they snapped directly to hers, realizing a little too late that I might have been too rough, too forceful. But the pride that shone in her eyes told me she had taken me like a champ.

"So how did I do?" She fluttered her eyelashes at me coyly.

"You want a grade? I thought you were the teacher?" I teased her, reaching out to take her hand and help her to her feet.

"I'm just a fan of feedback," she said. "You know, being a playwright, student and actress myself…I like to note areas for improvement. So, if you have any notes about my performance, areas to—"

I stood up and grasped her chin in my hand, pulling her toward me. "*Haud yer wheesht, lassie…*"

"What the fuck does that mean?" With a questioning blink, she drew back a few inches so she could see my face.

"It means 'shut up,'" I explained, "as in *haud yer wheesht and kiss me.*"

I didn't have to ask twice—she closed her eyes and angled her head, ready for my lips to meet hers. Once they did, she sighed, sinking into my embrace and surrendering to my plundering tongue.

It had been a long time since I'd thoroughly kissed a woman. It had been even longer since I'd felt this much of a pull toward one. As I tasted her on my lips, my cock grew hard again, raring to go as it pressed against her curves. I wanted to bend her over her desk, lift up her skirt and have my way with her right here.

I wanted to claim her as my own.

But she belonged to someone else. A woman. How would that work?

How would any of this work?

She pulled back, and my brain stopped churning out all this jumbled shite. "You good?"

She nodded, her lips visibly kiss-swollen despite her grin. "I can't believe I've never done that before. Thank you for giving me that experience, Lachlan."

"Thank *you*?" I repeated, dumbfounded. "I believe *I'm* the one who should be offering my eternal gratitude." I chuckled heartily.

She tilted her head, studying me. "This all feels so new to me…so forgive me if I get all twitterpated about it."

"'Twitterpated,' now there's a word." I sat back down in her desk chair and pulled her onto my lap, enjoying the way her curvy bottom pressed down on my stiff cock.

"I want to be honest with you. I tend to overcommunicate. Just ask Poe; she's always telling me silence can be golden."

"Smart woman," I agreed with a laugh.

"I just… I don't want to fuck up my show, but… I'm really enjoying getting to know you."

"Likewise." I didn't feel the need to add anything else to her confession.

"Did you give any more thought to the offer you had to go back to Scotland next semester?" She traced a tattoo on my forearm featuring the Scottish flag and a thistle, a symbol of my homeland.

I was surprised she'd remembered our brief conversation about the offer the other night when we went to Mother Bear's. After everything else that happened that night, I wouldn't have blamed her if it slipped her mind. But she'd been paying attention.

"Actually, haven't thought about it much," I admitted. "I'm trying to get through this play and the rest of rugby season first. I don't have to give them a firm answer for a few weeks yet." That was true. Hadn't spent too much time dwelling on it. I supposed I'd been a little preoccupied with learning my lines and getting to know a certain pink-haired lass.

"Gotcha…" Her voice trailed off, and her attention seemed to float away for a moment. Then she was back with me. "Plans this weekend?"

"Saturday is a rugby day," I shared. "That's about it."

"Would you want to come over to my place for dinner on Sunday? I know you've met Poe, but the rest of the polycule would love to meet you. And your roommate will probably be there too."

"Aye, that was an interesting turn of events. Darth's a bit of a nutter, *ye ken*? Sorry again about that scene in the kitchen the other night." I shook my head, remembering the look of horror on Molly's face when she saw him standing there.

I was surprised to find out they already knew each other. *Och, it's a small world after all.*

"So…Sunday dinner?" She pierced me with those mesmerizing green eyes, holding me captive.

I wanted to say no. Being with a group of people— even if I knew half of them—wasn't my idea of fun. And how could Poe possibly be okay with me having a bit of fun with her girlfriend? I didn't get this poly thing—what did she call it? A polycule?

"Lachlan?" She stood up, and my lap felt cold where her sweet curves had just been. "If you don't want to, it's fine. I just—well, I thought it might be fun for you to get to know my friends."

No clue where it came from, but before my head could stop my mouth from running off, I blurted, "I'll come to dinner on Sunday if, the weekend after, you'll go to my rugby mate's Halloween party with me."

Her mouth opened, but no sound came out at first. Then those parted lips spread into the biggest smile, and she said, "It's a date."

Another win, another drink-up. I wasn't Man of the Match this time, but I also escaped without a black eye or any other major injuries. Steve, our hooker, slapped me on the back when he welcomed me into the bar. "Here's a beer, man."

"Thanks, lad." I took it from him and imbibed a huge gulp. "Cheers!"

"Cheers!" rang out from my teammates.

"Hey, you comin' to my party next weekend?" Burke shouted from across the table. "You're gonna bring that hot waitress, right? Stephanie? I don't think she's working today."

"Naw, I have a real date." I moved down the table closer to him so I didn't have to yell. "We'll be there."

"Oh, yeah? Real date? Who's the lucky lady?" Sam was suddenly behind me, his hand on my shoulder. "Anyone we know?"

I hadn't told anyone about my role in Molly's play. No one. I wasn't about to spill that info here. God, I'd probably never live it down. "Met her at work. Molly is her name."

"Can't wait to meet her," Burke said. "What are you guys wearing?"

I stared at him, blinking.

"For costumes?" he prompted.

Shit. I supposed we needed to come up with something. I'd have to talk to her about that tomorrow at this dinner I'd somehow gotten roped into attending.

I shrugged. "Why don't you just consider yourself lucky that we're even coming?"

Burke, Sam, and Steve all burst into laughter, and then, thankfully, Steve changed the subject.

molly

"I'm nervous," I admitted as I made another lap through the house checking that everything was in place.

"You're making me nervous too, pacing like that," Poe complained. She stopped me in my tracks, raising her arms in front of me and blocking my forward motion. "Sit down and have some wine before you give yourself a panic attack."

"What if he thinks this is too weird?" I confined my pacing to the space right in front of the sofa.

"Molly, everything's going to be fine. It will be fun!" Cynda exclaimed, coming from the kitchen. She had just opened the oven door to check on the lasagna. The aroma wafted out and traveled right into my nostrils, its cheesy, garlicky goodness making my stomach growl.

"I still can't believe Darth and Lachlan are roommates," Jason piped up on his way out of the bathroom. "I asked Darth why he didn't say anything, and he said, 'I know him as Lan. So when you were talking about some Scottish guy named Lachlan, I really didn't put it together.'"

"Darth marches to the beat of a different drummer," Cynda said with a laugh as she joined us in the living room.

Jason started humming Darth Vader's theme from *Star Wars*.

Poe pulled me down onto the sofa, practically into her lap. *Guess my pacing is over.*

Sagan took off running down the hall like a lightning bolt just as the door handle turned. *Speak of the devil...* Darth appeared in the foyer and made his way to the living room, taking off his thick flannel shirt to reveal a gray waffle-weave Henley underneath. "This where the party's at?"

He looked like he was trying to be funny, but he came across as socially awkward. I was glad Cynda and Jason liked him, but he just annoyed me for some reason, and I couldn't quite put my finger on it. Clearly Sagan didn't like him, and animals were excellent judges of character. But that wasn't saying much because that damn cat didn't like me either, and I was awesome. At least Lachlan's sweet pup Bonnie Skye seemed to adore me. She had good taste—just like her owner.

"Is Lachlan on his way?" I asked him.

He shrugged. "Who?"

I rolled my eyes. "Your roommate?"

"Right. Lan. Um, no idea. Haven't seen him today."

I had texted him my address earlier, and he just responded with a thumbs-up emoji. He wasn't exactly the most communicative person on the planet—part of what made him perfect for the role of brusque, brooding Hamish MacGregor in my play. But it was a little frustrating to deal with in real life.

Of course, Darth was just as bad. I bet those two could

be under the same roof for days and never exchange more than a few monosyllabic grunts.

"I better get the lasagna out of the oven," Cynda declared, standing up. Darth didn't bother to sit down. He followed her into the kitchen like a puppy dog. Jason just smiled and stayed in the living room with us.

"Oh, Poe," I suddenly remembered, "I'm not sure why I forgot to tell you, but Lachlan invited me to a Halloween party next weekend—his rugby teammate is throwing it. Do you have plans?"

Her face brightened. "Actually, Delaney asked me if I'd want to catch a showing of *Rocky Horror Picture Show* with her. With the costumes and props and the whole nine yards."

Well, damn it. That sounded fun too.

"Okay, well, sounds like we both have separate plans for the night, then." Maybe we could go back to see *Rocky Horror* together a different night. It was one of my favorite shows.

She grinned. "Sounds like it. But we really need to plan a date night when your play is over."

"I can't believe my play is the weekend after that." I sighed and stood up. Then the pacing started all over again. If I couldn't be nervous about Lachlan, surely I could be nervous about the play. "We're totally off-book next week. I don't know if I'll survive."

"Molly, everything is going to be fine," she assured me for the four millionth time. She was a saint.

When a knock sounded on the front door, Jason sprang into action. "I'll get it." He puffed out his chest and headed to the foyer. My heart pounded as the doorknob turned.

Why was I so out-of-sorts about this dinner?! I didn't know if it was because this dinner was the first time I'd really put the "poly" part of my relationship to the test, or if I was nervous about everyone liking Lachlan. Or if it was because I was afraid Lachlan would find my polycule too weird and not want to entangle himself in something like this.

Or maybe it was because I really, really liked him. And didn't want to admit how much.

"You made it!" I greeted him when he stepped into the foyer. "This is Jason, Poe's brother."

He gave him a chin dip as Jason retreated toward the kitchen to stand next to Cynda and Poe.

"You already know Poe and Darth, and this is Jason and Darth's partner, Cynda."

"Great to meet you all," he said. "Thanks for having me."

I ushered him into the dining area. "I think we're about ready to eat. Cynda made lasagna."

"It smells delicious," he confirmed.

As we were taking our seats, I got a good, long look at him. He was wearing jeans and another concert t-shirt; this one was Alice in Chains. No black eyes this time, and his beard was a little fuller than before. We had discussed him growing it out for the play, so he must have decided to do that now. Every time I reminded myself we had less than two weeks until the play, I nearly collapsed, hyperventilating, to the floor.

Small talk around the table as we passed around the lasagna, salad, and garlic bread was…stilted. Cynda and Jason kept us going with their antics, but Darth wore a permanent scowl, Poe looked uncomfortable, and Lachlan…well, he just seemed to be taking it all in.

"You're quiet today." Poe's eyes landed on me as she scooted her chair away from the table. She shook her empty wine glass as the unspoken signal that she needed a refill.

"Sorry, maybe I'm a little tired from overthinking," I admitted, then immediately regretted saying that out loud. "About the play, I mean. I have scenes and blocking running through my head."

Poe came back to the table with the wine bottle and topped mine off. Then she put her hand on my knee as she took a sip from her refilled glass. "You, overthinking? Nah, that can't be right."

Everyone laughed. Cynda turned to Lachlan. "So what do you think of acting? Have you gotten bitten by the theater bug?"

He let out a deep chuckle. "No, I think I'm going to stick to behind-the-scenes type stuff after this. Not to say I'm not enjoying the experience, and Molly is an amazing director. But I don't think I was born to be in the spotlight."

"Look at us!" Cynda exclaimed, setting down her fork and dabbing at her mouth with a napkin. "Aren't we just the perfect example of kitchen table poly?"

I nearly choked on my sip of wine. I was really hoping not to dwell on the whole polycule thing, though I supposed that was impossible with Poe and Lachlan both here.

Lachlan cleared his throat. "I need to apologize—I haven't the foggiest idea what that means." He laughed a little as he glanced around the table.

"It's basically when your partners and metamours can all sit around the kitchen table openly like this," Cynda explained. "Metamour—well, for example, if you and Molly are in a relationship, Poe would be your metamour. It's your partner's partner, if that makes sense."

Lachlan dropped his fork onto his plate, making a clanging sound. "Oh, sorry. Didn't mean to drop it like that."

"Have you ever dated someone who is polyamorous before?" Jason piped up.

I wanted to crawl inside a box and never come out. Were they purposely trying to make this as weird as possible? What the fuck?

"I have not," Lachlan admitted.

"I hope we're not scaring you off," Cynda interjected.

"It takes more than that to scare me off," Lachlan said. "Remember, I play rugby—a sport just as physical as football but with no pads or helmets."

"Good point," Jason agreed, laughing.

I buried my face in my palms. Maybe *I* was the one who wasn't cut out for kitchen table poly.

"I'm learning a lot," he continued. "I appreciate how open you are with each other. That's admirable."

Poe elbowed me. "Again, do I know how to pick 'em or what?"

eleven

. . .

lachlan

I SAID goodbye to everyone at Molly's house and thanked Cynda for preparing the meal. "I'll walk you out," Molly said, shooting a look at her housemates that appeared to be a look of warning. For being so short and having a relatively sunny disposition, she sure could be intimidating when she wanted to be.

She closed the front door behind us and followed me down the porch steps to my truck. "I'm really sorry about that," were the first words out of her mouth.

I cocked my head and stared at her. "Why are you apologizing? Your housemates seem really nice. I'm glad I got to meet them."

She studied my face for a moment. In the dim light, her normally light green eyes looked the color of stainless steel. "I didn't want this to be weird for you…but I understand if it is."

"It's not weird so much as I'm not used to it," I admitted. "I think it's cool though. It's really cool that you guys can be so open and share and…"

I didn't mean for my voice to trail off like I was trying to convince myself of something else positive to add, but I knew that was how it came across.

It *was* weird, okay?

When you've grown up with monogamy as the standard, the ideal…and you've been told over and over again there's a soulmate out there for you… To just be patient, and that one woman who is meant to be yours will eventually materialize… I kinda figured it was bullshit since I was still waiting at thirty years old. And it wasn't for a lack of looking, either.

Even so, it was still hard to wrap my head around this notion that I didn't have to hold out for the one woman/one man standard that had been crammed down my throat ever since I could remember.

"I don't know exactly what's happening between us," Molly said, bringing my focus back to her. "But I do know I like you, and I have fun whenever I'm around you."

"Likewise," I confirmed.

Her head tilted as the tiniest smile lifted the corners of her lips. "And the idea of not being around you or seeing you…like when the play is over…"

Her words shot right through me. I didn't want to think about not seeing her. "It's hard to think past the play right now, isn't it?"

She smiled. "It is. I don't want to put any pressure on you. I just want you to know how I feel. That I like you."

"Well, the feeling is mutual, Ms. Rose." I reached for her hand and brought it to my lips, brushing her knuckles with a soft kiss.

"I guess I should let you go… I'd hate for you to use

me as an excuse for not having enough time to memorize your lines," she joked.

"*Och*, I see what you did there. Have no fear. I'll be working on that when I get home," I assured her.

"Promise?" She looked up at me, her smile crinkling her eyes. The chilly night air was turning her nose and cheeks pink, matching her hair, and stars danced in her eyes as they wordlessly beckoned me closer. I drew her into my arms, my lips finding hers as the sun sank into the tree line behind her house.

Her warm lips and tongue, the feel of her curvy body in my arms, something about it felt so right. So different from what I'd expected, from anything I'd ever experienced. How was this happening? Why was this happening?

And why did I never want to let her go?

"So, this party on Saturday…" Molly set her script down, and it became clear she had left director mode and was queueing up girlfriend mode.

Fuck, did I really just call her my girlfriend in a roundabout way? I'd be lying if I hadn't started to think of her that way. A part of me was excited to have her meet my rugby mates and even endure the onslaught of ribbing I'd likely get about her being a curvy pink-haired theater geek.

"Yeah? What about it?" I moved closer to her, checking to make sure all my castmates had strolled out of the theater. It was so frustrating when they lingered, talking and fucking about when all I wanted to do was make out with the director. I wasn't a patient man.

"Is it a costume party?" Her eyebrows arched. "You said it was a Halloween theme, right?"

"Yes. But we don't have to wear costumes if you don't want to," I assured her.

She scoffed. "Lachlan, I'm about to receive a master of fine arts in theater. Do you understand what that means? I've been happily dressing up in costumes for nearly my entire life. I would never, ever, in a million years miss an opportunity to dress up in a costume."

"*Och*, I didn't realize you felt so strongly about them, lass." Her serious expression made me want to laugh out loud, but I tried to restrain myself.

"You don't have to dress up, but I would certainly love to," she reiterated.

"I didn't know if you'd had time to find a costume," I explained.

"You don't understand, do you?" She shook her head. "I have half a closet of costumes at the ready. Pirate wench? Check. Medieval queen? Check. Fifties poodle skirt? Check. Witch? Triple check. Do you have a costume?"

I chuckled, the deep sound resonating in the empty theater. "Well...I've got a kilt handy, if you think that'd work."

Her eyes got this funny look, and she wiped her mouth. "Yes. Yes, please. Kilt please," she stammered.

"What'll you wear then, if I wear a kilt?"

"I'll figure something out," she assured me. "Now, I'd love to hang out, but I have to get home. Poe and I are having dinner with some friends of hers tonight."

"*Nae bother*, Molly. Hope you have a good evening.

Walk you to your car?" I was secretly hoping to talk her into coming by my house tonight, but I supposed that wasn't going to happen.

"Sure, of course. Parked close today. Got lucky." She gave me a wink before she gathered up her things and slipped into her coat. She was wearing a ruffled skirt over leggings and her combat boots tonight, and I really wanted to go investigate the curves being concealed by those ruffles. *Another time…*

I followed her down the stairs and out into the burgeoning twilight. I guess we'd stayed later than I thought, and the days were getting shorter. "We call this time of day 'the gloaming' in Scotland," I shared as we hiked up the hill to the car park.

"Gloaming, that's an interesting word. I'll have to remember that." She stopped beside her car and looked up at me, expectation in her eyes.

I knew she expected a kiss, but I wanted to give her so much more. "So, yeh wanna see me in a kilt, do yeh?"

"Oh, yes. Definitely." Her smile glimmered in the fading daylight as she looked up at me with fluttering lashes.

"I'm really looking forward to sharing it with you," I said. "Hope you have fun with your friends tonight. See you tomorrow at practice?"

"Of course." She smiled and lifted up on her tiptoes, anticipating my lips against hers.

I didn't make her wait. I cupped her face in my hands and leaned in, brushing my mouth to hers slowly, softly at first, and then more insistently. Her lips parted for my tongue, letting it twirl against hers before my teeth nibbled at her bottom lip. She gasped at the contact as I held her to my body, tightly enough for her to feel my arousal straining against her.

"Feel what you do to me?" I rasped in her ear. "This weekend, I hope that kilt will make your panties fall off so I can be with your naked body."

Something between a sigh, gasp and a giggle erupted from her mouth, and her head flew back, exposing her neck. I took a nibble and a taste, making her go weak in my arms. "I wanna be inside you, Molly. I wanna make you come on my cock."

She moaned when my teeth found the delicate tissue of her earlobe. "Fuck, Lachlan…"

"Exactly." I gave her one more kiss and then left her standing by her car, too speechless to respond.

"Aye, my Bonnie lass, I love yeh too. Now let's go do yer business, lassie, *ye ken*?" I opened the back door, and my sweet little girl bounded out into the chilly October night. While she was watering her favorite spot on the lawn and leaving a present in the fall leaves at the edge of the woods, I walked over to the detached garage and peered in.

I hadn't done any tinkering in the garage since the summer. I'd been so busy with work, rugby, and this play, I hadn't really thought about what my next project would be. But right now, my hands were itching to build something, to feel the power of the tools flow through me. I was burning to create something, to start with nothing, and then, at the end, have something tangible in my hands to show for my hard work and ingenuity.

"C'mon, Bonnie Skye." I whistled to capture my girl's attention. She ran over to me, my sweet black fluffball, and followed me inside the garage. It was cold in here, and when I turned on the light, I noticed everything was covered in a fine layer of dust. I had a pile of scrap lumber and a new box of wood screws. What could I get myself into tonight?

I rubbed my hands together. I had just the thing.

molly

"That was fun," Poe said as we drove back home after dinner. "Marta and Jocelyn make such a cute couple, don't they?"

"They do. Did you say they're poly too?" I turned onto the street that would take us most of the way home and promptly got stopped at a red light.

Poe tilted her head. "Oh, no. Not at all. You didn't catch what Jocelyn said?"

"I guess I didn't. What did she say?" As soon as the light turned green, I was off, pretending to race the Honda beside me.

"She said something about how she didn't like it when they went out, and someone has the nerve to flirt with her girlfriend right in front of her. She said men are especially bad about hitting on Marta when they're out in public," Poe explained.

"Well, can you blame them? Marta is hot with that long red hair and legs for days. I can't blame them for trying!"

"Jocelyn has made it very clear she has no intention of sharing her," Poe continued.

"Why, were you thinking of making a move on her?"

"Well, she is gorgeous. And that accent…"

"Where did you say she is from?"

"Austria," Poe said.

"I should be able to remember that. Marta is one of the Von Trapp family singers, and they're from Salzburg, Austria." I rolled to a stop at yet another red light. College Avenue was full of them, and they didn't seem to be timed very favorably.

"Of course you would make a *Sound of Music* reference in relation to our dinner date." Poe sighed. Then she changed the subject. "Did you and Lachlan work out costumes for the Halloween party you're going to?"

I reached over and grabbed her hand, squeezing hard in my excitement as I squealed, "Yes! He's wearing a kilt!"

"Well, try not to sound so excited about it!" Poe teased me. "And what are you wearing, Miss Costume Warehouse in Your Closet?"

I scoffed. "Hey now. I don't have that many. Probably only a dozen or so."

She laughed and smacked my arm. "I think you're underestimating."

"Well, anyway, I have a renaissance faire costume I think would go nicely with his kilt, so probably that. Corset, peasant blouse, skirt with bloomers underneath."

"Sounds sexy. You're definitely getting laid, you know that?" She patted me on the thigh.

When I turned toward her at the next light, I saw a glimmer in her eye. "You think so?"

"Yeah, you may not even make it to the party!" She laughed, and then the sound faded away. It was quiet for a moment.

"What's wrong?" I turned down our street.

"Oh, nothing. Just wishing…"

"Wishing what?"

"Do you know anyone who's going to be at this party?"

"I don't think so." I shrugged. "It's his rugby teammate who's hosting it. So probably not."

She sighed again and looked out the window. I pulled into our driveway, and she was still staring at something outside the car.

"Poe, tell me what you're thinking about, babe." I laid my hand on her thigh and stroked up a few inches, garnering her attention. "What were you wishing? Do you not want me to go to the party?"

"No, it's not that. Not at all. I like Lachlan and think you guys are so cute together," she insisted. Then there was a pause as she seemed to gather her thoughts. "I just wish I could go to a Halloween party with you as a couple. A real couple. And I could grope you in public and kiss you and stuff."

I looked down at my feet. "Well, I really doubt Lachlan and I would do anything in public. Like I said, I don't know these people..."

"But Lachlan does," she pointed out. "And if you're drinking and dancing and having fun, who knows what might happen?"

We both got out of the car and made our way inside. It was dark now, and the half moon was looming in the sky, spilling light and creating shadows across our front yard.

"I want you to go," Poe said when we reached the front door. "So please don't take it the wrong way. But...I just... Well, I'm excited for being able to go out in public and really be *out*, you know? A couple. With you. I've gotten a taste of it with Delaney because she's out, and she's not from around here anyway, but... I'd like to have that with you too."

"You know we can go out any time you want," I reminded her. "It's not like I don't claim you."

She folded her arms across her chest. "I mean as your girlfriend, and you know that's what I mean."

I tried the handle, and it was unlocked. Cynda and Jason must be home. I pushed the door open, but let Poe enter before me.

"I know. And if it wasn't for my family and everything being so strained—and my inheritance from my grandfather..." I sighed. "We'll be heading to New York soon. If this play goes well, we might be going this summer."

She captured my gaze with her pleading eyes. "And then, that's it? Once we're settled there, you won't care if your family knows about us?"

"I will shout from the rooftops that I'm in love with a woman," I promised her. I pulled her into my arms and pressed my lips to hers. "And not just any woman—one Poe Elizabeth Davis. I promise."

twelve

. . .

molly

IT WAS UNSEASONABLY warm in southern Indiana today, about seventy-five degrees. Not to worry. It would probably snow next week. Such was Midwestern weather. I smoothed out my voluminous skirts, thinking about how hot I was probably going to get once I started drinking.

Walking up the steps to the porch, I sucked in my gut in my corset. I didn't think Poe could have laced it any tighter. It was like a sudden wave of sadism washed over her when she was helping me get ready.

Hopefully, my date would appreciate my efforts. The plan was for me to leave my car at Lachlan's so we could ride to the Halloween party together. I brought an overnight bag just in case.

When I rang the doorbell at Lachlan's house, I was expecting Lachlan to answer the door. He did not. It was Darth.

Ugh.

"Moving in?" Darth watched me through the screen door, making no move to invite me inside the house.

I rolled my eyes. "Is Lachlan here?"

"He took his dog on a run and then decided to take a shower." Darth still stood there, arms crossed over his chest.

"Well, do you mind if I come in and have a seat while I'm waiting for him?" What was this guy's problem? I couldn't understand what Cynda saw in him, but maybe he just really hated me.

"I guess." He shrugged. Then he walked away from the door. Sigh.

I opened it and looked around. I didn't see where Darth went. I didn't see Lachlan, and I wasn't being greeted by Miss Bonnie Skye either. Curious. I took a seat on the sofa and waited.

I didn't have to wait long because, as soon as his bedroom door opened, a furry black streak of lightning bolted down the hall and was in my lap licking my face in a heartbeat. "Well, hello to you too!" I tried to protect my makeup, and, you know, my face in general, from the slobbery attack.

Footsteps sounded, barely audible over the little dog's pants and whimpers. When I looked up, Lachlan was standing before me in nothing but a towel. I gulped.

His tattoos glittered with droplets of water, and his hair and beard were shiny and wet. His stormy eyes fell on me as I stood up, setting his dog on the floor. I stood to my full height as his lips parted, his tongue darting out to lick his bottom lip.

"Fuck, Molly... We aren't gonna make it to the party, are we now?"

I couldn't think of an answer to that because my eyes

were too busy taking in his beefy pecs and biceps. *Drooooooooool!* I wanted to lick all the excess water off him —that might at least take the edge off my thirst.

"Sorry I'm running late. My lassie needed a good run before she's cooped up all night with the likes of Darth," he explained.

I felt bad for her too. "No problem. Um, do you want me to wait here while you get dressed?"

"Nae, I wanna have a look at yeh." He reached out and took my hand, twirling me around. "Your breasts are magnificent, Molly."

I did notice his gaze kept going right to the girls, and they were on full display in this purple brocade corset. "What time does the party start again?"

"Let's not worry about that right now, shall we?" He extended his hand, and once I grasped it, he led me down the hall to his bedroom. Bonnie Skye followed along like she was part of our little parade.

"Sorry, *wee bairn*, not right now," he *tsked* as he shut the door before she could come in.

I heard her whimper softly outside the door. "Poor baby."

"She'll be okay." He guided me to the center of the room, where he flicked his wrist and made a show of dropping his towel. "*Do yeh see what yeh do tae me, lassie?*"

His thick cock jutted out, tiny droplets of water glittering in the dark reddish-brown curls surrounding it. I had a momentary flashback to that scene in my office last week and how good he felt in my mouth. Without another thought, I dropped to my knees, looking up at him with a submissive stare.

"Fuck, Molly...you look so fuckin' sexy on your knees

like that. I haven't cum since that time in your office when you drained my balls."

"No?" My tongue darted out to lick a quick stripe up his shaft, and it made him shudder.

"My balls are aching, Molly. And my cock is so fucking hard. You remember what I said to you at your house on Sunday night?"

"You said you wanted to be inside me," I remembered.

"Aye…so consider this just an appetizer…"

I didn't say a word, just wrapped my lips around the tip before sliding my mouth down as far as I could. He was just too big and thick to take the whole thing, so I needed my hands to help. One cupped his heavy balls, and the other stroked up his shaft. I looked up just in time to see his eyes roll back in his head.

I didn't get very far before he lifted me up. "How do I get this thing off ya?" He gestured at my costume.

"Carefully," I warned him. He gave me the slightest nod, his stormy gray eyes filled with desire as I slowly unclasped the busk at the front of my corset, freeing my breasts as his tongue darted out again to lick his lips. I laid it carefully on the chair across from his bed, then released the skirts and stepped out of them. I was wearing only a pair of purple lace cheeky panties and knee-high brown leather boots.

"Holy shit, yeh look amazin' in yer boots an' knickers." He stood there for a moment, seeming to drink in the sight of me. I had never felt so sexy as I did under his piercing gaze.

My cheeks flushed crimson as he stepped toward me like a predator—a starving predator. I'd seen flashes of his intensity when he was in character as Hamish MacGregor, but offstage, he'd always been fairly mellow. Not now.

Now he was a wolf stalking his prey, and that prey was me. His eyes turned almost silver as they locked on to me, making me shiver as much as his touch when his thick fingers ran down my shoulders to my hips and then around to squeeze my ass and pull my body to his.

I had never been fully naked with a man before him.

Ever.

Those times in high school, we always had some clothing on.

I thought I'd be mortified. Self-conscious. But the lust in his penetrating stare filled me with confidence. And while I was secure in my own body, I was wary of what he would do next...because that stare bordered on dangerous.

lachlan

The blush on Molly's cheeks screamed of innocence, though I knew she wasn't, not really. She just wasn't accustomed to having sex with men. I kept reminding myself I should go slowly, ease her into it, but every cell in my body was urging me to stake my claim, to bury myself deep inside her.

With practiced patience, I traced the curve of her cheek, her chin and down her chest to one breast, cupping it as I bent my head to tease her peaked nipple with my tongue. When she let out the softest moan, I sucked it into my mouth and lightly bit into the tender flesh. The gasp that slipped out of her mouth sent a thrill right to my cock.

I didn't think it was possible for it to be any harder but... that sound certainly proved me wrong.

After lavishing attention to one breast, I turned my focus to the other until the sounds coming from her were on the verge of driving me mad. I pushed her down onto the bed, kissing down her stomach until I reached the apex of her thighs. Then I struggled to pace myself before all-out feasting on her soaking wet pussy.

Her legs tensed as I licked a stripe all the way up her slit to her swelling bud. She shuddered when my tongue swirled around it, so I backed off, sliding a finger between her folds until I breached her entrance. I groaned when I realized how wet she was, her juices gushing out around my fingertip.

"Fuck, Molly, are you ready for me?"

"Yes," she whimpered. "I want your cock inside me, just like you promised."

"No, I need to make you come first," I decided. "No cock until you come. Those are the rules."

Her head fell back onto the pillows as I hummed against her clit, exhaling my hot breath and eliciting a sigh. I teased her opening again, this time with my tongue, before delving inside and gathering her juices and swallowing them down.

Fuck, she was going to be the end of me.

She was so wet, so responsive, and as I started to lick and suckle at her clit, her back arched, her hips thrusting rhythmically into my face, rocking against my mouth. Once I learned the rhythm she needed, I slowly slid two fingers inside her, stroking her G-spot until I thought she might fly off the bed.

"Oh, god, how do you do that to me?" she ground out as she continued to buck against me. "That's it, slow and deep like that." Her fingers threaded through my hair as her panting intensified. Seconds later, she detonated with a resounding, "Oh my god, oh fuck!" that likely carried all the way into the woods.

I let her ride the waves of ecstasy until she was no longer a quivering mass under me, then I slid up her body to straddle her, one leg on either side of her hips, and my rock-hard cock resting on her mound. I only had to lean forward and reach for my bedside drawer to grab a condom. With hooded eyes, she watched me roll it down my shaft.

"I want to fuck you now, Molly," I warned her. "It's been a while for me, and I haven't been this fucking turned on for—well, maybe ever—so I can't make any promises as to my stamina—"

She shook her head. "Don't worry about that." Her hands wrapped around my waist, pulling me forward. "I want to feel you inside me…please…"

I lined the tip of my cock up with her swollen lips and closed my eyes as the searing heat of her flesh soaked into me. Holding my breath, I slid inch by inch inside her, watching her face for signs of discomfort. Every expression that touched her features was one of anticipation and pleasure.

"Oh, god, Lachlan…you feel so big…"

"That's about half," I groaned, trying to restrain myself from slamming home. "Are you okay to take more?"

"Yes please." She opened her eyes and met mine, biting her lip with a mix of minx and innocence.

I didn't hesitate. I pushed forward, my cock sinking into her as a sigh hissed out of her mouth. As I began to slowly stroke inside her, her hands moved from my waist to the sheet on either side of her, which she gripped in her fists as she pushed up to meet each of my thrusts.

The resulting sensation was so deep, so intense, my balls tightened, and I squeezed my eyes shut, desperately trying to hang on to a shred of control. I wanted to make it last long enough for her to come again, but I seriously doubted my ability to do that.

"Lachlan, my god, this feels so amazing. You're so fucking deep…"

"I know," I grunted out, "I don't know how much longer I can last." I leaned back and moved my hand to her pussy, feeling our connection where my shaft breached her entrance with each slow rock of my hips. My finger brushed her clit, and she jerked and bucked up to meet my hand again, so I continued to rub in circles as her body tensed under me.

From the way her face twisted up, her lips parted and nothing but soft pants slipped out, I knew she was getting close. I rocked a little deeper while still stroking her clit, and she shouted as her walls suddenly tightened and waves of spasms began to milk my cock. I couldn't take it any longer. As her pussy sucked me in deeper, I picked up speed, draining my balls in a loud, primal grunt.

My climax crashed over me, stealing my balance, and I collapsed on top of her. As her own orgasm died out, her arms wrapped around me, her gentle words of encouragement coaxing me as her pussy wrung every last ounce of cum from my cock.

"Fuck, Molly, that was –"

"Shhh…"

I closed my mouth, my eyes and just rested my head on her heaving chest as the only sound filling the room was us catching our breath.

The whole time we were at the party, I considered grabbing Molly's hand and whisking her off to a private locale so I could ravish her body again. My cock turned to granite at the thought of being inside her again. How was I going to make it through the night?

I'd gone without sex with a partner for several months, but now that I'd had Molly, it was like my cock had awakened. Now every other thought I had was about making her pussy milk it again. And every time she looked up at me, those green eyes seemed to admit we were sharing the same thoughts.

"Hey, Burke, this is quite a turnout. I didn't think you knew this many people," I teased my mate when Molly went to use the restroom.

"I didn't think you could get a woman to come with you," he joked back, elbowing me in the ribs. We'd both had a few beers at this point, so we were feeling loose and well on our way to being fully sloshed.

Molly wormed her way through the crowd assembled in the kitchen preparing to do a round of shots and made it to my side. "Are these all rugby players?"

"Oh god, no." Burke shook his head. "A lot of these guys are my work friends, and my sister is here somewhere. She invited her friends too. You can tell who they are because they're the prudish ones not drinking."

I laughed. "Oh, you mean the people in the living room? What are they doing? Playing Monopoly or something?"

Burke laughed and shook his head. "Euchre."

Molly rolled her eyes. "My family loved playing Euchre. Me, not so much."

"*Och*, I know that game!" I slapped my knee. "Used to

play it with some English fellas at camp when I was a lad. It's been ages. I didn't know they played it around here."

"Oh, yeah, big Indiana thing. All over the Midwest," Burke explained.

"Maybe I can get in on a game." I rubbed my hands together. "Do you mind, Molly?"

"Whatever floats your boat. I'm gonna grab another drink first."

I leaned down and planted a kiss on her cheek. "I can wait for you."

"Nah, go ahead. I'll be fine," she assured me.

I gave her a kiss on the lips for good measure, then Burke and I made our way through the crowd into the living room. Everyone was starting to relax their costumes —masks were long discarded. Makeup was a bit smudged. I saw various costume accessories strewn around the living room: belts, swords, a couple of wigs. In the center of the cramped room, a card table was set up, and four people were in a heated battle.

I stood beside one of the guys, looking at his cards. I hoped I remembered how to play. It didn't take long before they finished.

One of the ladies stood up and announced, "That was fun, but I gotta pee. Anyone want to take over my spot?"

I lifted a finger, volunteering, and she gave me a soft smile. She had dark brown hair and eyes, and was on the pleasingly plump side. The woman next to her had dark hair and pale skin, and was dressed as Little Red Riding Hood in a white dress with a red cape over it. The guy next to her wore a flannel shirt and his wolf mask was sitting on the shelf behind him. The other player was a stocky balding guy with glasses and, from what I could tell, a Harry Potter costume.

I plopped down. "I'm Lanny. Haven't played this game since I was a lad at camp, so go easy on me, will ya?"

"Cool accent. You from Scotland?" the Big Bad Wolf asked. "I'm Eli, by the way."

"Aye," I gave my standard answer. I was to be Harry Potter's partner. "I'm guessing your name's not Harry?"

He chuckled. "Brandon. Nice to meet you."

"I'm Meredith," Little Red Riding Hood informed, shuffling the deck. "Nice to meet you, Lanny. How do you know Burke?"

"We play rugby together," I explained as she started to deal out the cards.

A few seconds later, I looked over my shoulder at the entrance to the living room, and Molly was standing there with her mouth gaping wide open. "Molly? What's wrong?"

She didn't even look my way. Her gaze was zeroed in on Little Red Riding Hood. "Meredith?"

thirteen

. . .

molly

I STOOD there for probably thirty seconds—or it might have been an eternity—but all the players were absorbed in looking at the hands they'd just been dealt. Then Lachlan glanced over his shoulder at me and found me frozen.

"Meredith?" tumbled out of my mouth as I stepped forward, my eyes locked on my sister. "What are you doing here?"

She turned to me, a huge smile lifting her cheeks. "Molly!" She set her cards facedown on the table and leapt up to envelop me in a hug. "I didn't know you'd be here! How do you know Burke or Bekka?"

"You guys are sisters?" came out of Lachlan's mouth before I could say anything. My heart pounded—as far as my family knew, I didn't date. "Molly came with me." My grumpy Scotsman actually fucking grinned.

I couldn't believe it.

Meredith's jaw nearly dropped to the table. "You're

with Lanny? That's so cool! We were just getting to know him. Why don't you pull up a chair? Love your costume— wow, Molls, that's really sexy." She nearly blushed when she said the S-word which was probably foreign to her pure little tongue.

Fuck. Fuck. Fuck. I stood frozen until someone shoved a chair under my ass and pulled me down into it. I remembered the drink in my hand. I needed to make use of that STAT.

My sister was dressed as Little Red Riding Hood, and her fiancé as the Big Bad Wolf. "Hi, Eli."

I gulped down another sip of my whiskey sour. Next drink, I was holding the "sour."

"Nice to see you again, Molly. Do you play euchre?"

"No, she hates it," Meredith answered for me as their game got underway. I was glad they were playing, though, because it gave me a chance to stew.

Lachlan and his partner won the first round, and then Meredith yawned. "I'm not used to staying out this late!" She giggled and batted her eyelashes at her fiancé.

It was eleven.

"I'm going to go get some water. Anyone want anything?" She stood up and stretched. "Molly, wanna come with me?"

I sighed, knowing I wasn't going to like this conversation. Surely they'd be leaving soon, though. Didn't they have to go to church in the morning? She wouldn't want to be the heathen daughter who didn't show up for services under the watchful eye of her pastor father.

"You don't seem like the party type," I said to Meredith as she grabbed a bottle of water from the cooler.

"I'm not," she conceded. "But we figured, what the

heck, it's fun to dress up sometimes, right? I guess with you being in the theater, you're used to it, huh?"

I nodded and smiled. "I didn't think you even celebrated Halloween?"

"Well, I don't really…" She took a sip of her water. "How long have you been dating Lanny?"

I wanted to steer very clear of *that* conversation, so I continued interrogating her. "Do Mom and Dad know you're here?"

She shrugged. "Well, I am an adult, you know. I figure it's none of their business."

I nodded, impressed. "You're right about that. Only a couple more weeks and you'll also be a married woman."

"Are you guys serious?" she pressed. "Oh! Oh! This means you'll have a date for my wedding! Whooo hoo! Will he wear his kilt?"

My head immediately began to ache as I scrubbed a hand down my face but desperately tried to maintain my smile. "Uh, well, I—"

She was entirely too excited. "Oh, you have to bring him! He seems so cool!"

We were joined moments later by Lachlan and Eli. "We should go soon, honey," her fiancé said. "Sunday School starts at nine, you know. It's going to come early."

Lachlan flashed me a horrified look, and I rolled my eyes.

"I was just telling Molly that I'm so happy she has a date for the wedding!" Meredith gushed.

"Wedding?" Lachlan's eyebrows arched.

"Oh, my sister and Eli are getting married the weekend after the show," I explained, then reached down into the cooler for my own bottle of water. I needed something stronger, because that last drink didn't seem to do jack squat for me, but I also felt I should probably keep my wits about me before my sister got me into all kinds of trouble.

"You'll come, won't you?" Meredith reached down and grabbed Lachlan's hand, pulling on it like a small child begging their mother for a treat at the store.

"It's not the same weekend as the play, right?" Lachlan's brows quirked again as he looked at me. Why did he actually look excited about this prospect?

I was not ready for this. Not at all, and my parents? I wouldn't wish them on Lachlan. And what would Poe say? She wanted to go to the wedding with me so bad. She wanted us to be a couple.

How could I just show up with Lachlan and pretend like I didn't have a girlfriend I was madly in love with at home?

"We'll have to talk about it, won't we?" I said firmly, then I shot Lachlan a look I use to convey I mean business when I'm directing.

"Sure, of course." Lachlan smiled and also grabbed a bottle of water from the cooler.

"Well, Eli's right. We probably better get going since we have church in the morning. Don't want to get on Dad's bad side. Especially when he's paying for the wedding!" She laughed and threw her arms around me, kissing me on the cheek. "I'm so glad we ran into you guys," she whispered in my ear.

Right before she turned to leave, she patted Lachlan on the shoulder. "So glad we got to meet. Hope to see you at the wedding!"

Oy. I had some damage control to do.

lachlan

I watched Molly's sister and her fiancé file through the crowd and exit out the back door. Molly started to head toward the living room, but I grabbed her hand, whipping her around to face me. "Are you okay?"

She shrugged. "Yeah, why wouldn't I be?"

"Um, you didn't seem very happy to see your sister," I noted.

She closed her eyes briefly and blew out a breath before looking up at me. "I'm fine."

So, she was going to ignore my observation.

"If you don't want me to go to the wedding, nae bother," I said. "You probably want to take Poe anyway."

She shook her head. "It's loud in here… Do you want to go outside? It might be quieter out there."

"Aye, alright." I guided her through the crowd in the kitchen, and we stepped out onto the back porch, which was covered. "Nice out here. What do ya say?" I gestured toward a wicker loveseat, and she nodded.

She sat down, and I plopped onto the cushion next to her. "Look, my family is—"

I held up my hands. "No one understands family issues better than me."

Her head cocked. "Is that so?"

"Well, why do ya think I have an ocean separating me from mine, then?" I mirrored her, tilting my head to study her features in the moonlight spilling onto the porch. She was so gorgeous illuminated in the silvery bands of light— she looked like a goddess.

As she wrung her hands in her lap, I realized her emotions were seeping into me. I was feeling her pain, her heartache. Her family—it was a painful topic for her.

I understood how families shaped one's actions, beliefs, and dreams. I understood how the people bound to you by blood could fail you, disappoint you. Disrespect you. Trap you in a box and not free you once you'd outgrown its confines.

"So, how about this?" The moon spawned a gleam in her eye as her gaze roamed my face. "I'll tell you why my family is fucked up, if you tell me why yours is fucked up."

"That sounds fair." I had to chuckle at the way she was bargaining with me. "You first."

She sighed. "I think I told you that my family is religious."

I rested my hand on her leg. "You said your dad's a man of the cloth?"

She nodded. "Yes. But you have to understand—my whole family is very traditional. They believe homosexuality and premarital sex and celebrating Halloween—and, fuck, a whole lotta other things—are sins."

"Oh, so that's why you asked Meredith if they knew she was here?" It was starting to become clearer to me why Molly was the proverbial black sheep of her family.

"Right." Molly put her hand on top of mine. "They don't know I'm bisexual. They don't know I'm in love with Poe, or that I'm polyamorous. They think she's my roommate. Our relationship is…fragile…"

"Got it," I assured her. *Och*, I understood precarious relationships with the clan.

"I'm trying to hold things together for Meredith's wedding," she continued. "But also trying to keep my private life a secret. There's a lot of pressure on me to get married, settle down, pop out some babies—come back to the church. Oh, I mean married to a man, of course."

"Of course."

"I don't have any intention of doing any of that," she confirmed. "But I don't want to rock the boat right now because, two years ago when I first started grad school, my grandfather died. My mom came from money, and he left each of us grandkids a decent sum. Meredith is using hers to buy a house."

"Damn, must've been a good amount!"

She laughed. "Yeah, I mean, it's not enough for the whole house, but it's enough for a really big down payment, and it's also financed my master's degree. Plus, I plan to use the rest for getting started in New York—"

"That's right, you said you plan to move. I love New York," I added, though I wasn't sure why I felt the need to tell her.

"Right, hoping I can make some connections and get my plays produced." Her eyes sparkled with dreams. "Anyway, that's it. Just trying to keep the peace. If they find out my true relationship with Poe, I will probably be disowned and lose access to the rest of my inheritance, since it's in a trust fund controlled by my parents. The money was actually left to my mother, but she's doling it out to Meredith and me. I probably should take a date to the wedding. It would keep her off my case for a while."

I squeezed her hand. "I would be happy to accompany you, but I don't want to piss Poe off."

"Right, there is that. I'll have to talk to her." She let out a long, frustrated sigh. "Okay, your turn."

I stood up, rubbing my hands down my thighs as I tried to figure out how to phrase everything. It seemed silly compared to her complaints, and I was lucky enough to be thousands of miles away so I didn't have to deal with them.

"You don't have to tell me if you don't want to," she insisted. She stood up from the loveseat and made her way over to me. The cool northerly breeze turned into a sudden gust, lifting the pleats of my kilt.

"Nice ass." She stood behind me and reached underneath, running her hands up my bare thighs to my bum, which she squeezed. "So firm. I kinda wanna smack it."

I let out a little chuckle. "Is that so? Well, dinnae let me stop ye."

I looked over my shoulder in time to catch her grin as she lifted the fabric up, exposing me to the cool air. I grabbed on to the post as she reared her hand back and brought it down firmly on my bare ass cheek. "Damn! That stung!"

Now I needed retribution. I knew she was only wearing a pair of lacy knickers, so I whirled her around and plopped her down on the loveseat in one fluid movement. Then I pulled her down until she lay over my knee. Lifting her voluminous skirts, I ran my fingers up the back of her leg until I found the curve of her lace-covered backside.

"My turn," I announced, and I didn't waste any more time before bringing my palm down hard on her soft flesh, eliciting a yelp.

"Fuck!" she squealed. "Do it again!"

My hand came down hard again, making a pleasing slapping sound. I looked all around, trying to ascertain if we were being watched. God, I wanted to take her right here on the porch with the cool autumn wind whirling around us, but it didn't seem like a good idea.

"Come on." I lifted her to her feet, and she shot me a confused look. I grabbed her hand and stood up next to her.

"What? Where are we going?"

"I need you." I pressed her hand to the front of my kilt, and her eyes widened.

"But, where are we—?

My finger rose to her lips, and I shook my head. She nodded and wordlessly followed me down the porch steps and into the black of night. It was nearing midnight, and the party was still going full force. Surprisingly, there didn't seem to be any other party-goers outside, which was perfect for my plan. I knew Burke's property pretty well as he'd hosted a couple of summer barbecues out here, and there was a pole barn behind the house. It was kept rather neat and orderly—almost obsessively so, as it contained his prized collection of antique tractors.

The side door was unlocked. I flashed a devious smirk over my shoulder at Molly, who watched me turn the handle with a mixture of surprise and delight on her face. "There are windows, so I don't want to turn on the lights, but, here—" I whipped out my phone, turned on the flashlight, and set it on the workbench that ran along the same wall as the door.

"Wow, it's pristine in here." She spun in a circle to take it in. "I've never seen so many tractors in one place."

"Haven't you ever been to a summer fair?" I teased her. "I'm not even from here, and I know they always have a tractor pull at the county fair."

"Oh, right. Guess I never paid attention. Too interested in the funnel cakes, corndogs and fried Twinkies." She shrugged, and in the dim light, I could barely see a smile lift the corners of her mouth.

I pulled her over to one of the bigger tractors. It was old but had been refurbished with one of the newer cushioned seats, not the old metal kind that would hurt your ass after a few minutes. I climbed on board and bounced up and down, assessing its sturdiness for what I had in mind.

"What the fuck are you doing? Fulfilling some sort of weird farmer fantasy?" she teased me.

"Get up here. You're gonna sit on my cock." I grinned as I lifted my kilt, and the monster sprang up like a jack-in-the-box, pointing straight to the ceiling.

Her eyes widened, and her head shook back and forth. "What? No…that doesn't seem like a good idea."

I bit my lip as I gripped it and slowly stroked my shaft. "This cock needs attention, Molly. It's craving your hot, wet pussy, and I want ya sitting on it now."

"Or what?" she goaded me.

"Or else I'm gonna take you over my knee again, and this time, I'm gonna leave marks."

She cocked her head as her fists flew to her hips. "That doesn't sound like much of a deterrent to me."

I threw my head back with a sigh and squeezed until a bead of pre-cum appeared on the tip of my cock. "I'm not gonna beg ya, Molly. But I will take matters into my own hand—"

I didn't finish my sentence before she began climbing aboard the tractor. Reaching out a hand, I helped her climb the final step onto the platform where the seat was perched, then I held her steady as she mounted herself on my lap. She stood up, her feet on either side of the seat, and slowly lowered herself to my cock.

"Condom?" she gasped right as her lips grazed my engorged flesh. The sensation sent a shudder through my body.

I wordlessly reached into my sporran and grabbed a condom. I might not've been a Boy Scout growing up outside Edinburgh, but I knew how to come prepared. Seconds later, it sheathed my throbbing cock, and I was pulling her down to sit on it.

I watched her face as she lifted her skirts and took me inch by inch. Her lips parted until her teeth sank into her bottom lip and her eyes fluttered closed. A look of bliss enraptured her features as she sat flush against my thighs, her hands on my shoulders.

My own hands traveled to her hips at the edge of her corset, lifting her and then slamming her back down against me, her soft ass smacking against my balls. Fuck, this was so hot—knowing we might get caught made it even more so.

I yanked her breasts out the top of her corset, and she thrust forward, allowing a nipple to be caught between my teeth. "Fuck!" she yelped when the pain mixed with pleasure shot through her, squeezing me hard as it traveled through her body.

"That's it, *mo leannan*, ride my cock. I wanna feel that pussy milk me dry, Molly. Be a good girl and give it to me faster now." I pumped up inside her like a piston as I went back to teasing her nipples.

"Yes, oh my God, yes, oh, fuck, Lachlan, I'm gonna come," she rasped as she continued to slam down onto me, her full skirts rustling against my thighs with every bounce.

I tightened my grip on her hips and sped up even more, my lungs squeezing in my chest as heat flooded my skin. She felt so fucking good, I never wanted to stop, but I had an ache deep in my balls that forced me to explode inside her at the same exact time as the walls of her pussy began to flutter and contract around me.

"Fuck, Molly, you drained me again." I held her as she

rested her head on my shoulder, equally spent. And for some reason, all I wanted to do was take her home, take her to bed with me, and let her sleep in my arms till morning.

For some reason?

Who was I fucking kidding?

I knew the reason.

I didn't like the reason, but it didn't make it less true.

I was fucking falling for her.

fourteen

. . .

molly

THE DRIVE back to Lachlan's place was quiet. I worried he was upset about something—I didn't know what, though, because he seemed to enjoy himself in the pole barn. But after he came and we both readjusted our costumes, he said he was ready to go. It was not even one o'clock yet. I'd told Poe not to wait up, but she probably wasn't even home from her date.

He turned off the truck, and I gathered up my purse. "Well, I guess I'll head back to my place, then. I had fun at the party. Thanks for inviting me."

I started to climb out, but he grabbed me by the wrist. "Please…" was all he said.

I shifted in the seat to look at him. "What's wrong?"

He swallowed hard, his Adam's apple bobbing. "Is there any chance you can stay the night?"

My heart thumped wildly against my chest as I considered his request. "I'll have to call Poe—not for permission, exactly. It's just our agreement, if we change the plans, we always check in first."

"Nae bother either way." He patted my hand. "But I'd love for you to stay."

"Give me a sec." I smiled and opened the truck door so I could climb down. The sound of the doors latching shut filled the cold night. "I'll be right in, okay?"

He nodded and headed for the house. I pulled my phone out of my purse and dialed Poe. While I was waiting for it to connect, I heard Bonnie Skye's excited greeting, and then he brought her outside on a leash to do her business.

"Hey…" I said when Poe's soft voice said hello.

"You okay? What's wrong?" were the next words out of her mouth.

"Nothing's wrong. I just want to know if you care if I stay the night?" I thought about all the times she had stayed the night with various women she'd dated. She didn't do it often, but there had definitely been a handful of times over the past few years.

I had never asked. Not once.

"Oh, sure, that's fine. Actually, I was going to see if you minded if I crash at Delaney's place tonight anyway. I didn't want to bother you at the party though," she admitted.

"Oh, well, as Lachlan would say, 'nae bother.'" I laughed. "We are home from the party already."

"You are?" She sounded surprised.

"Yeah…I…" I didn't want to tell her about running into Meredith. I'd save that for in person. I didn't even want to think about it myself right now. "We had fun though."

"That's good. I'll see you in the morning, babe. I love you."

"I love you too." I hung up and started up the stairs to Lachlan's porch. If I thought I was nervous to fuck him, that was nothing compared to how nervous I was to stay the night.

Did this mean things were getting serious?

"Well? What's the verdict, Director?" Lachlan joked from the kitchen as I joined him. He was pouring white wine into two long-stemmed glasses. Bonnie Skye rushed over to say hello, and I bent down to give her some love.

"Thumbs-up!" I reported, taking the glass he offered. The wine tasted sweet and bubbly as it hit my tongue. "Mmm, this stuff could be dangerous."

"No danger except falling into bed with a handsome man in a kilt." He winked and gave a little pelvic thrust.

"That doesn't sound dangerous to me—more like a dream come true." I laughed as I took another long sip. "Have you given any more thought to taking the bio department up on their offer to work in Scotland for the semester?"

I kept telling myself that a semester wasn't that long, and I didn't want to influence his decision. He should go home on the university's dime.

What if he didn't want to come back, though?

He lowered his gaze to his wine glass, swirling the liquid around a few times before he looked up at me. "Still haven't decided. Being that close to home is…well…"

"You never did tell me about your family," I reminded him. "You don't have to, of course. But I have to admit I'm insanely curious."

He ran his fingers through his hair and then continued scrubbing them down his face. "It's so embarrassing…*ah dinnae ken*, Molly."

"You don't know?" I repeated, laughing at the reddish

color creeping into his freckled skin. As a ginger—even though his hair was darker than most redheads—his coloring gave away his embarrassment. I found it absolutely adorable. "I think you need more wine. Or do ya got anything stronger?"

He chuckled and tossed back the rest of his wine. "Prob'ly do." He pulled out a bottle of whiskey from a lower cabinet, grabbed two shot glasses out of an upper cabinet, and poured a generous amount in each. "C'mon, lassie, drink up."

"How many words do the Scots have for being drunk?" I quizzed right before it was down the hatch.

"*Och*, too many. We're still inventing them, *ye ken*."

"Okay, back to your family. So it's not something bad, then? The way you were talking before, you made it sound like something truly horrible."

"It is horrible!" he insisted. "But more horrible for me than anyone else." He sighed and grabbed my hand, nearly dragging me into the bedroom. Bonnie followed, her metal dog tags making a clinking noise as her little feet carried her over the threshold.

"Give me a minute." He pulled open his closet doors and began rummaging through a box in the bottom of it. "I cannae believe I'm showin' this to ya."

I noticed that the more time I spent with Lachlan, the more his accent came out. I didn't know if it was because he was used to speaking his lines as Hamish MacGregor in a thick accent, or if it was because he had grown comfortable with me. I believed it was at least partially the latter, or he wouldn't be sharing something embarrassing with me, would he?

He tossed a large photo album on the bed. When I opened it, I saw it was actually more of a scrapbook, the kind that was popular back in the 90s and early 2000s. "Wow, this is really cool!"

"My mam made it for me," he explained, "when I graduated from…well, they'd say 'high school' here."

The first page had absolutely stunning landscape photos. "Is this Scotland?" Each picture was postcard-quality.

"Aye. That's Isle of Skye—where Bonnie's name comes from. We used to go on a family vacation there every summer. That's the Old Man of Storr." He pointed to a rather phallic-looking rock formation with the bright blue ocean in the background.

My eyes nearly bugged out of my head. "Holy shit, that is fucking majestic! You got to see that every summer?"

He nodded, seeming a little choked up at the sight of his Motherland. "Turn the page."

When I did, there was a shot of five young men posed in front of the towering rock. "Is that you?" I pointed to one of the taller boys, one with reddish hair.

"*Och nae*, that's my brother James." He pointed to the picture. "These are my brothers: James, Callum, Finn, Graeme, and me there on the end."

"Wow, that's you?" I squinted. He looked tiny. Scrawny. "How old are you there?"

He pinched the bridge of his nose like it was painful for him to admit. "Fourteen, I think. Maybe fifteen."

"Seriously? I would've guessed like ten years old!" I stared at the photo again. "Your brothers are all older?"

"Nae, that's the embarrassing part. I'm the second-oldest."

"What?!" I was shocked. "You're all close in age, then?"

"My brothers Callum, Finn and Graeme are thirteen,

eleven and nine in this picture." He sighed. "So…I was always tiny when I was growing up, and I got bullied a lot. My family was the worst, to be honest. My brother James, the oldest one there, he's seventeen in that picture. He did the most damage to my ego. He started calling me Pipsqueak when I was about ten. It stuck."

I could tell the memories of it truly upset him, but I found it so sweet and endearing. "Awww, that's not so bad, Lachlan! Look at you now. You're a big, beefy dude! How did that happen?"

He stood up and started pacing. This still bothered him a great deal, even twenty years later. Having also been teased about my size when I was growing up, I needed to be more understanding.

"You don't understand. Even my teachers called me Pip. I didn't top five feet until I was twelve. At sixteen, I was about five-four and a hundred twenty pounds soaking wet. And then, all the sudden, puberty happened."

"At sixteen?"

He nodded. "My voice squeaked; my face was loaded with acne; hair started sprouting everywhere. It was absolutely excruciating," he revealed. "And then…"

"Then?"

"Then I got accepted into the foreign exchange student program. You probably wouldn't believe it, but I was a nerd. Super fuckin' smart. When I came over to the States, I knew I could be whoever I wanted to be. No one in America would know they called me Pipsqueak. So, I went to the entirely other end of the spectrum…"

"You mean sexy rugby player?" I guessed.

"Nope. Turn a few pages… See?"

I flipped through pages of what looked like photos

from his time with his exchange family. There was a picture of him at the Indianapolis 500, and one at what looked like Conner Prairie. Another showed him in a Purdue hoodie. "I'm gonna pretend I didn't see that one," I teased him, as Purdue was my alma mater's biggest rival.

"Wait, is that you?" I flipped to the next page, and there in front of me was an unrecognizable goth kid in full makeup with jet-black hair and piercings everywhere. He wore wide-legged black pants with multiple zippers and chains hanging off them and a black t-shirt with skulls and some band name I'd never heard of.

"Aye. After my weenie phase, I went through a goth phase. It started to cover the acne. When you wear makeup and have all those facial piercings, people don't really notice the zits," he explained.

I stared in shock at the photos. "Oh, wow. I can't believe that's really you! Looks like you finally grew though."

"I shot up from five-seven when I first came to Indiana to almost six feet by the time I went home. I was there for a year before I came back for college, and I grew a little more. But I kept the goth for a while."

"Everyone has embarrassing stuff they did in their youth," I assured him. "You should see some of the shit I wore."

"You mentioned your family being religious," he said. "Mine was fairly traditional too. My mam told me at least once a day that I was going to hell when I was there for my last year of school."

"Well, that we do have in common." I patted him on the back. "Don't you think they'd be over it if you saw them now? They wouldn't still make fun of you, would they?"

He shook his head. "Nae, prob'ly wouldn't. But that's not the point, is it? I hated my family. I hated the way they patronized me and made my life a living hell, Molly. And that's why I'm not too keen on going to Scotland, even though I miss my bonnie homeland so much."

I squeezed his hand. Despite our earlier glass of wine and shots, we both seemed completely sober now. "I'm sorry your family treated you that way. That they didn't accept you as you were."

"When I told you I understood not being accepted, that's what I was talking about." He sighed like he was trying to cleanse his palate from the unwanted memories.

I nodded. "I get it. I also relate to being bullied. I was bullied about my weight all the time growing up. And you saw my sister. She's tiny. My mom always went on and on about how cute her figure was." I rolled my eyes. "I got sick of hearing that all the time."

"I can imagine." He tossed the scrapbook on the chair by his bed and swept back the covers. "I do have one rule in my bed, lassie."

"Oh, yeah?" I arched an eyebrow as I watched him strip off his shirt and remove the furry pouch-looking thing from his kilt. "What's that?"

He pinned me with his stormy gaze. "No clothes in my bed. Got it?"

I smiled. "I think I can live with that rule."

"Off with them, then." He clapped his hands together, and seconds later, he let his kilt drop to the carpet. He was completely naked underneath. Talk about incentive!

I unfastened my corset and my skirts and stepped out of them. Then I slid my lace panties, which were still soaked from my earlier arousal, down my thighs and tossed those onto my pile of clothes. I was so glad I'd packed an overnight bag—just in case—and I wouldn't have to put those back on in the morning.

Lachlan patted the mattress. "Shall we?"

I climbed into bed, and he pulled me into his arms. "Are you tired?"

"Completely knackered," he answered. "You?"

"Same." I rested my cheek on his firm pectoral muscle as he draped his arm around my waist and tugged me closer.

"I'm glad you came with me tonight, lassie."

"Me too."

fifteen

. . .

lachlan

THE SUN WAS STREAMING through the blinds, and a furry butt was sitting on my chest when I woke up. Before my eyes blinked open, it was lick, lick, lick, right to my mouth. Just when I was starting to think Molly's kissing skills had seriously deteriorated overnight, I realized Bonnie Skye's tongue was the one assaulting my face.

"Shhh, *wee bairn*, let's go out now." I slid out of bed, my eyes trailing over Molly's sleeping form. She was facing away from me, and I could only see the luscious curve of her hip and a shocking tuft of pink hair against the tartan pattern of my flannel pillowcase.

I grabbed my fur baby and headed out to the kitchen, where I fastened her lead to her collar. As soon as she was finished doing her morning business, I served her breakfast, hoping it would occupy her while I snuggled back up with my other beautiful lass. After washing up a bit— especially the dog slobber from my face—I climbed back into bed.

Wrapping my arm around Molly's waist, I yanked her backward into my naked form. "Aaaack!" she moaned as her heat soaked into my cool flesh.

"Aye, you're so warm…" I nuzzled into her neck, feeling the blood flow right to my cock, making it stiffen against her voluptuous ass cheeks.

A muffled reply came from beneath the covers. I cozied up, pressing my hard-on right into her asscrack.

"Oh my god," she squealed. "Well, that's one way to wake a girl up."

"Mmm, feel what you do to me?" I thrust into her again. "I need to be inside you…what do you think?"

"I mean, I'm not going to say no, though I am still kind of asleep over here…"

"I'll do all the work," I promised her. "Let me just suit up." I reached behind me for a condom and slid it on before probing for her pussy.

When I slammed home, she screamed, "Oh, fuck, Lachlan!"

"Are you awake now?" I growled into her ear.

She pushed her ass toward me, taking my cock deep. "Mostly awake, yes."

"Yer pussy feels so fucking tight, lassie. I'm not hurting you, am I?"

"No, sir." She shook her head for emphasis.

"Mmm…say that again…"

"What? Sir?"

"Aye…very nice…yeh keep takin' my cock like such a good girl, I'm goin' tae come so hard."

"Is that so?" She pushed back against me even harder, nearly making me lose control. I reached around and grabbed both of her breasts, squeezing her nipples roughly.

"Oh, fuck, now if you do that, you're gonna make *me* come," she threatened.

"Well, that's not much of an incentive to stop now, is it?"

"No, sir," she quipped and seemed to be stifling a giggle.

"That's it. On yer knees, lassie." I pulled out, smacked her ass, and lifted her off the bed.

She complied instantaneously. "Yes, sir."

"There's my good girl." I ran the tip of my cock down her asscrack, teasing her back hole. "Ever taken a cock here?"

"Not a cock...but a toy, sir," she obediently replied.

"I want to take you here next time we fuck," I warned her. "Be ready for me."

"Yes, sir."

I teased her pussy lips apart with the head of my cock then reached around to stroke her clit. "You want me inside you again?"

"Yes, sir."

I bit my lip to suppress the growl that rumbled deep in my throat, but I was sure she still heard it. I teased her hole again as she arched her back and whimpered. She was so fucking sexy!

"Please, sir," she begged, grinding against my cock. "Please fuck me."

"You want this cock?"

"Yes, sir," she rasped, and I slammed home, causing a wild scream to erupt from her mouth.

"Fuck." Now that I was inside her, there was no way I was going to be able to hold back my orgasm. My fingers dug into her hips as I pounded into her pussy.

"Lachlan," she groaned, "oh...god...yes!" Her whole

body tightened, and then she threw her head back, a string of garbled curses flying off her tongue.

I gathered her pink hair in my fist and picked up a punishing pace, hammering into her so fast, she had to grip the headboard to keep from flying off the bed. "Oh god, ohhhhh fuck…goddamn…" I exploded inside her, my rhythm gradually slowing as each wave of my climax carried me to another level of ecstasy.

She finally looked over her shoulder at me, my first glimpse of her face this morning. There was such a serene look of satisfaction painted on her features. I ripped off the condom and threw it in the bin, then slid up the mattress to take her in my arms.

Neither of us said a word. She just lay in my arms, her soft breath falling on my chest.

I was in trouble. So much trouble.

I wanted to wake up like this every morning.

But it wasn't possible, was it?

molly

I drove away from Lachlan's house feeling warm inside despite the chilly autumn air. As I approached our street, the orgasm high started to fade, and reality began setting in. I wondered if Poe was home yet because I really needed to talk to her.

Relief coursed through me when I saw her car in the driveway. I parked behind her and hurried inside. Sagan gave me a nasty scowl as I let myself in the back door. Voices in the living room carried down the hallway, so I bypassed our bedroom and went to see who was up and about this early in the morning.

"Well, look who the cat dragged in!" Cynda exclaimed from the sofa, where she was curled up with Darth on one side of her and Jason on the other. Relief filtered through me—that meant Darth wasn't there this morning when Lachlan made me scream.

"He didn't drag me in, but he sure gave me the stink-eye," I joked about Sagan, who had just roamed into the living room, saw how crowded it was and backed the fuck out with a twitch of his whiskers and a flick of his tail.

"We wondered when you were going to show up," Poe said from the recliner in the sofa. "Sleep in this morning?"

"Kinda," I answered, but as soon as the word came out of my mouth, a blush began creeping up my neck. When was I going to learn how to control my body's reaction every time I thought about Lachlan's cock inside me? First, I remembered the tractor incident, and then this morning's romp flashed through my mind.

"Looks like Molly's in L-O-V-E!" Jason exclaimed before taking a sip of his coffee.

I flashed him a nasty look since Darth was sitting right there. I was all for kitchen table poly, but I also respected Lachlan's privacy—and my privacy, for that matter. Also—coffee. That was what was missing from my life.

I ignored his comment and headed into the kitchen to fulfill my need for caffeine. I would be able to think clearer once I'd downed a cup or six. At least I hoped so.

"You didn't have a snappy reply for my observation?" Jason started in when I returned to the kitchen. "Go on, finish your coffee. I'll wait."

"We had fun at the party," I chose to ignore his L-O-V-E comment, "but there is a problem."

"Problem?" Poe's eyebrows arched, and she shifted in

her recliner, looking ready to spring into action in case my problem necessitated it.

I plopped down in the recliner on the other side of the room. "Well, you'll never guess who was at the party."

"Who?" everyone asked in unison.

"My sister!"

I was expecting more shock and awe, but everyone was kind of like, "Oh, cool."

"No, not cool," I insisted. "She met Lachlan."

"So?" Jason cocked his head, then looked around as if checking to see if he was the only one who didn't see an issue with this development.

"So…she went on and on about how she couldn't wait to see Lachlan as my date at her wedding in a couple of weeks." I breathed in deeply and ran my fingers through my hair. With my play approaching so fast, this was the last thing I needed to worry about. It was next weekend, for fuck's sake! We had a few run-throughs, and then opening night was Friday.

"Oh." That was the single word out of Poe's mouth. I could tell from her face that she wasn't happy about it, and I decided now was not the time to discuss it in front of everyone. I turned to her and smiled. "How was your night with Delaney?"

"Wonderful!" She seemed unable to repress the glowing smile that spread her lips at the thought of her new partner. "*Rocky Horror* was amazing. We have to go sometime and do all the props and stuff."

"I'd love to. I did it once a long time ago, but it would be fun to go with you." I remembered going with my first girlfriend back in college. "And you spent the night at her house?"

She shook her head. "Actually, had her over here since you said you were staying at Lachlan's."

"Oh, okay." Seems like she should have told me that before, but whatever. We'd all sort of played the night by ear.

Cynda stood up and stretched. "Well, we better get on the road if we're going to get a hike in, boys."

"Oh? Where are you guys off to?" I asked as Jason and Darth flanked her.

"Brown County," Jason supplied. "Darth's never been."

"Well, that's almost criminal." I smiled, thinking of the popular Southern Indiana destination for viewing fall foliage. But Darth just scowled at me. Why did he hate me so much?

Cynda seemed to read the room, understanding intuitively that Poe and I needed to chat. As soon as they scurried back down the hall, Poe turned to me.

"So, did you guys boink or what?" There was no judgment in her tone, just curiosity.

"Yeah, you could say that. I mean, I probably wouldn't use *that* word." I laughed.

She scoffed. "Writers!"

"Look, I know the wedding thing upsets you…" I didn't miss the way hurt flickered across her features as soon as I said the word "wedding."

"You can't help it if your family is homophobic." She sighed. "I also know what's at stake with your trust fund."

I met her hazel gaze. "You want to move to New York, don't you?"

"I feel like you're trying to make a bargain with me." She stood up and walked over to the window. It was nearing noon now, and the sun was reaching its zenith in the sky. Wind rustled leaves on the trees, making them fly through the air in a shower of red and gold.

I came up behind her and wrapped my arms around her waist. "Is that such a bad thing? I thought relationships were all about compromise?"

Before she could answer, my phone rang. I yanked it out of my pocket and saw that it was my mother calling. She only called when something was wrong.

My first thought was that the late church service had just let out, and something may have happened to my father. "Sorry," I mouthed to Poe as I pressed the button to answer. "Hello?"

"Molly, hi, honey, how are you?" she practically cooed into the phone.

"Is something wrong, Mom?" I paced back and forth in front of the window as Poe sank back down onto the recliner, a sour look on her face.

"Can't a mother just call her daughter to see how she's doing?" The patronizing tone in her voice made it click instantly in my brain: my sister had told her about meeting Lachlan.

Of course, that would mean Meredith had to come clean about attending a Halloween party. Wouldn't put it past her.

"I'm doing fine, Mom," I said as evenly and patiently as I could.

"I'm so glad. We're in the middle of last-minute wedding preparations here. Are you busy today? I thought maybe you could come help us finish the centerpieces? If you have any friends available, I'd love their help too. Don't you have a couple of roommates?"

I let out a long sigh, which garnered Poe's attention. She glanced up at me, a questioning look on her face.

"I'm available," I admitted. "I'm not sure what Poe and Cynda are doing today, but I'll find out."

"If you can come over this afternoon, maybe around two o'clock, Meredith and I would be ever so grateful." Her voice was so sugary sweet, it made my teeth ache.

"Okay, Mom. See you then."

I hung up and slid the phone back into the pocket of my leggings. "Wanna come help my sister and Mom finish the wedding centerpieces?" I let out a humorless giggle. "After spending the afternoon with my mom, any desire you had to attend my sister's wedding will likely be quashed."

She rolled her eyes. "Well, I was hoping to spend the day with you."

I smiled. "If you come help, I'll take you out for dinner afterwards?" I sweetened the deal.

Poe rolled her eyes. "I guess that's one bargain I can get behind."

I gave her a peck on the lips. "Thank you, love."

She pulled me into her arms. "You can do better than that." She pressed her lips against mine and licked the seam of my lips.

I sank into her embrace and surrendered to her probing tongue. We might as well get this out of our systems before our afternoon at my parents' house…

lachlan

"C'mon, lassie, let's go." I fastened Bonnie's harness and attached her lead. She pranced down the steps and across the lawn toward the garage. I opened both wide doors and tethered her to the stately oak tree next to the garage. She loved being outside while I worked.

I hadn't had a lot of time to work on my project this past week, and time was running out for me to complete it.

I couldn't wait to see the look on her face…

sixteen

. . .

molly

MY PARENTS and sister had met Poe before, but it was sort of in passing. They'd never had uninterrupted time to grill her, evangelize her, and say all the things I'd prepared her for but was still horrified to watch playing out in front of me as I tried to quickly assemble the parts of each centerpiece.

"How did you and Molly meet?" my mother quizzed as she unpackaged another box of pearls.

"Uh, I don't remember, it's been so long now. Molly?" She turned to me, flashing a look that screamed "help!"

"We met on campus," I shared. "I was looking for a place to rent. Poe's brother Jason and his girlfriend Cynda own a house and were looking to fill some of the rooms. She was moving in with them too." Okay, part of that was true.

My mother became even nosier. "Are they married now?"

"No, not yet," Poe admitted reluctantly.

"That's too bad," my mother tsked.

I knew she was thinking about how they were "living in sin" and was barely biting her tongue hard enough to prevent a sermon about premarital cohabitation from spewing out. I shot Poe an apologetic look, but she didn't even look up from where she was hot-gluing a strand of pearls around a vase.

"How about you, Poe? Do you have a boyfriend?" my mother continued her interrogation.

Poe tucked a strand of hair behind her ear. "No, no boyfriend."

I flashed her a warning look.

"Pretty girl like you?" my mother continued. "I find that hard to believe. Why doesn't anyone your age want to get married and settle down anymore? I just don't understand it." She sighed and opened another baggie of glue sticks.

I could tell Poe's patience was teetering on the brink of annihilation, so I changed the subject. "Did you and Eli have fun at the party last night?" I asked Meredith.

Now it was her turn to shoot me a nasty glare. "It wasn't so much a party," she said, "as a gathering, right? Always fun to have a big euchre tournament. That's so cool that Lanny knows the game."

"Yeah," I played along, "not only did he learn at camp when he was younger, but he played with his host family in Fishers when he was an exchange student."

"So, he's from Scotland?" my mother asked. "Meredith said he was wearing a kilt! Will he wear one to the wedding as well?"

"Mom, I don't know if he's coming," I stated as firmly as possible.

"Oh, he said he wanted to come!" Meredith piped up,

then she shot me a conspiratorial smile. "He said he'd see me there."

"He did not!" I insisted. When I looked over at Poe, she seemed highly attuned to her work, like she was trying to ignore the conversation.

"Have you met him, Poe?" my mom pressed.

"I introduced them," Poe answered.

She gushed, "Oh, how exciting! How did you meet him?"

"He works in my building. He's going to star in Molly's show." My girlfriend flashed me a nervous look.

"Your show?" My mother's mouth gaped open. "Have you set a date for it? I don't know anything about this. What is it? When is it?"

Oh, lovely. I did not expect this can of worms to be opened. Guess I didn't warn Poe that my parents didn't know much about my thesis project. "It's next weekend." *Should have lied*, I berated myself after the words slipped out.

"Wow!" My mom shook her head. "You didn't even tell us! Is it possible to get tickets?"

"I mean, I guess so." I shrugged. *Fuck. Thanks a lot, Poe.* It wasn't her fault, but still. I didn't want my parents there.

"So do you like this guy?" my mom asked Poe.

"Yeah, he's great," my girlfriend answered. "Perfect for Molly." She didn't look at me. I knew she wasn't jealous of him—she was only jealous of his "acceptability" to my family.

"Does he have a brother?" my mom joked, her eyes crinkling. "Maybe you can date him?"

Poe's cheeks flushed. "I like girls," she said in a low voice.

Oh, great. Fuck and double fuck.

"Oh." My mom snapped her mouth shut.

Annnnnd that was the end of my mother's meddling for the afternoon. I changed the subject immediately. "So, Meredith, is your one bridesmaid, the one who's pregnant —did she have any trouble finding a dress?"

"Oh, no," Meredith said. "Sara got a flowy one with a stretchy waist. She'll be fine. I just found out my friend Autumn is preggers too!"

"Autumn's husband is going into the ministry," my mother said as if it were the best news ever. "It will be your turn soon, Mere." She turned to me. "Your sister and Eli want LOTS of babies, don't you, darling?"

"Well, we may have different definitions of lots. Two is fine." She giggled and set the centerpiece she had just finished aside. She stood up and began counting them. "Oh! We got so busy talking, we made two extras."

"Good! You never know, one might break," my mother pointed out. Poe finished hers and came over to stand beside me. "Thank you so much, girls, for helping us out. Many hands make quick work, isn't that what they always say?"

"Something like that. Thanks for having me, Mrs. Rose." Poe extended her hand to shake my mother's.

I expected her to say something like, "Please, call me Jane," but she didn't. She shook my girlfriend's hand and then turned to tell my sister something.

"Let's get out of here." I put my arm around Poe and led her to the front door, but my dad stepped right into my path.

"Molly, leaving already? I barely got to see you," he said.

"Guess you should have helped with the centerpieces,"

I joked, trying to keep my tone light. "I'll see you the weekend after next at the wedding."

"What's this I hear about you bringing a date?" The corners of his lips turned up at the prospect of me being "normal."

"It's not set in stone. Have a good week, Dad!" I reached out and patted him on the shoulder.

He opened the door for us. "Have a good evening, ladies."

We both walked stiffly to my car, which I unlocked with the key fob before we climbed in. Once the engine was rumbling and my Broadway tunes were flowing, I turned to Poe, whose face was buried in her hands.

"I'm so fucking sorry, Poe. I'm so sorry." I shook my head as I backed out of the driveway. She didn't utter a word. "Where do you want to go for dinner? I'll take you anywhere you want to go."

"Mexican," she said with a tiny sniffle. "I need carbs, cheese, and tequila. Not necessarily in that order."

"Mexican it is."

lachlan

I stood in the spotlight during our first dress rehearsal. It was the end of the second act, and I was delivering a speech to Ruth, the woman who had saved me from a life in prison and with whom I'd fallen madly, deeply in love.

The spotlight was bright, but not bright enough to blot out the playwright and director's pink hair from her spot front and center in the audience. Knowing she had penned these words gave them an entirely different meaning. Were these words she hoped would be spoken to her someday?

Were these words that had already been spoken to her,

and she had merely borrowed them to immortalize in her art?

Whatever the case, I was delivering the speech to Ruth, but in my heart—the words were being spoken to Molly.

"So I'm a free man?" my voice boomed into the silence as I turned to face my savior.

"Free as a bird," came Ruth's reply.

I paced forward, standing on the edge of the stage. "When I escaped, I knew there was only a small chance I'd live to tell the tale. Running equals guilt in the eyes of the law. In the eyes of a judge, a jury. And maybe a part of me *is* guilty," I admitted, letting that line hang in the air for a moment to shock the audience.

"Guilty of being in the wrong place at the wrong time. Guilty of never living up to my potential. Guilty of never believing I deserved to be happy. Guilty of thinking I would never find someone who accepted me for who I am…"

I turned to Ruth, walking toward her as I delivered my next lines with her in my arms, but in my peripheral vision, I kept Molly in view. "There is no way I could ever repay you for believing in me. Or being my rock. Or fighting for me when no one ever had before. All I can do is pledge my undying love and devotion to you and hope it will be enough to keep you in my arms forever."

Ruth turned to me with tears shining in her eyes. "Oh, Hamish—you deserve all the good things. And if one of those good things is me, then I'm the luckiest woman on earth."

I grasped her face in my hands and pressed my lips to hers. I'd practiced this scene with Kady, the actress playing Ruth, dozens of times, but Molly's director's notes usually said I needed to put more emotion, more passion into the kiss. So tonight I pretended Kady was Molly, and I gave it my all.

"And…curtain!" Molly stood from her place in the audience. The lights were still dark but for the spotlight on me. Kady walked off the stage as soon as the scene was called. Frozen in the beam of light, I watched a tear trickle down Molly's cheek as she beamed with joy. All I wanted to do was wipe that tear away, even if it was a happy one.

"Good work tonight, everyone!" Molly called. "Devon, can you go hit the lights?" Moments later, we all squinted in the sudden brightness. Except me. I'd been standing in the brightest light of them all for the last several minutes.

We gathered around as Molly delivered her notes from our dress rehearsal. In general, her impressions were positive. There was one scene she wanted to run through at the top of the following night's practice. I told my castmates goodbye when we were dismissed and watched everyone gathering up their belongings and making an exit between the rows of bleachers framing the stage.

I wondered if everyone knew Molly and I had developed a "thing," or if they were oblivious college students so wrapped up in their own little worlds, they didn't know or care. I hoped it was the latter.

"Well, Boss?" My eyes trailed over her curves as she approached the stage. "Any other feedback for me? Did I emote enough?"

"Well, you made me cry, so you tell me." She rolled her eyes then smiled. "You've come a long way. I'm so proud of you. And so grateful for your help!"

"I never thought I would end up liking it," I admitted, "but I did."

"I'm glad to hear that it wasn't completely unpleasant," she joked.

"Having a beautiful, sexy director might have had something to do with my enjoyment factor." I pulled her into my arms and pressed a kiss to her lips. "I have a confession for you too."

"You do?" Her green eyes lasered in on mine. "Do tell."

I leaned down and cupped her face in one hand. "You told me I needed more passion when I kiss Ruth at the end —so I just pretended she was you."

"Oh, my." She waved her hand in front of her face like she was hot and bothered. "That just sent a zing right down to my…lady parts."

"Mmmm…" I pulled her close to me, close enough she could feel my hardening cock straining against her. "You've got time for a quickie, right?"

"I have a meeting in my office I have to get to," she said with a serious look on her face.

"At seven o'clock?" I looked up at the clock on the wall at the back of the theater.

She laughed and leaned close to me, whispering in my ear, "A meeting with a certain sexy Scottish actor. No, not the late Sean Connery," she teased.

Her warm breath fanned against my ear before she sank her teeth into the lobe. My dick was already hard, but now it was like a steel rod.

"Better not be late!" I grabbed my jacket while she gathered up her script, notebook, and purse. Then I followed her out of the theater and up the stairs to her office.

She unlocked it and flipped on the light. I noticed she'd cleared the small couch by the window that was usually full of books. "*Och*, planning ahead?"

"Maybe?" She flashed me a devious grin as she started to pull off her fuzzy purple sweater. On the bottom, she was wearing a ruffled knee-length skirt with white daisies on a black background. And of course, the ubiquitous boots.

"I have to finish up a project I'm working on tonight—it's a surprise—so I can't stay long." Shit, I wasn't going to say anything, but I could hardly help myself.

Her head cocked, and her eyebrows arched inquisitively. "So you're gonna just fuck me and run?"

"I'll make it up to you after the show," I promised.

"Oh, *after* the show. Does that mean I'll still be seeing you after it's over?" She awaited my response, her thumbs hooked in her skirt ready to pull it down.

"I want to see as much of you as you'll allow me to," I admitted, leaning in to press kisses against her neck. Then my fingers explored her glorious cleavage before reaching around her to unhook her bra.

"Good answer, Kilt Boy." Now completely nude, she whirled around and bent over the edge of the two-seater sofa. "Now fuck me."

"Damn, woman, so bossy!" I unzipped my trousers and released the beast from its confines. It felt so thick and heavy in my hand, and pre-cum was already leaking out the tip. I ripped open the condom package and suited up.

I'd wanted to plunder her ass the next time I fucked her, but there was no time for that, unfortunately. What I wouldn't give for another full night with her—and not one we'd spent getting pished at a party. I needed a solid week of nights—maybe a full month of nights—to do everything to her I wanted to do.

I reached between her thighs and stroked down her slit. "Already so fucking wet for me…"

"I'm giving you a pass for foreplay, Lachlan." She

looked at me over her shoulder. "When I say I want your cock inside me now, I mean now."

Who was I to argue with that?

"Be careful what you ask for," I warned her as I parted her lips with the tip of my cock and then pushed my body forward, thrusting inside her with one rough stroke. I knew she was going to scream, so I had the foresight to wrap my hand around her mouth and muffle the wild sounds she was making as I drilled deep inside her.

"God, your pussy is so unbelievably wet and tight," I groaned as I continued to pound into her.

Unable to respond with words, she moaned, her hot pants falling on my knuckles as I held her firmly in place. My other hand reached around her to tease her clit, causing her to buck wildly against me, attempting to take me even deeper.

I was not going to last very fucking long in this scenario. And when she yelled out that she was coming—which sounded something like "Mmm-cmmmmng!!!" through my thick hand over her mouth, stamina was an even less likely prospect.

"Fuck, Molly, oh god, yeh want my cum inside yeh or somewhere else?" I gritted out between clenched teeth, trying to hold back long enough to give her some options.

"My mouth," I was pretty sure I heard her say.

I pulled out, and she whipped around, plopping down on the sofa cushion as I ripped the condom off. She opened her mouth, and I aimed for it, thick ropes of cum landing on her nose, her cheeks, her lips. I had never seen a more beautiful sight than Molly's face drenched with my seed.

We both stood there for a moment, me letting the last waves of my orgasm crash over me, and her licking the cum off her lips. As soon as I was able to move, I grabbed the box of tissues from her desk, pulled a few out and dabbed at her face.

"That was so fucking hot," she praised me as I tossed the tissues in her rubbish bin. "Come here."

"God, you came, and you're still bossy!" I chuckled as I sat down next to her, my trousers still unfastened.

She leaned against me, laying her head on my shoulder. I opened my arms and pulled her against my chest, wishing we had more time, more space, fewer clothes—well, for me. She was perfect in all her curvaceous glory.

"I wish we had more time," she said, almost as if she'd read my mind. "Seems I'm always thinking that."

"Spend the night with me after our opening show?" I suggested.

"Yes," she nodded, smiling, "yes, I'd like that."

seventeen

· · ·

molly

LAST DRESS REHEARSAL before opening night. To say my nerves were buzzing with a mixture of excitement and apprehension was a massive understatement. My heart felt like a rocket awaiting takeoff to the moon, full to the brim of propellant, just waiting for ignition. I left my office at a quarter till four and headed down to the black box theater, hoping everyone was on time, so we could get our run-through over with and have the evening to relax and prepare for Friday night's show.

I was surprised to find the theater's double doors were propped wide open. A loud commotion filled my ears—it sounded like...construction? But that couldn't be. If someone was messing with my stage, I was going to freak the fuck out. I had the theater scheduled all weekend. The next MFA student's show was the weekend after mine. The theater was booked solid for the next month prior to the end of the semester.

My mind swelled with racing thoughts. Why was someone trying to fuck with me?!

I couldn't suck in a full breath as I rushed down the corridor and into the theater. What I saw nearly stopped my heart.

A crew of men were nailing and drilling together a... set! It was enormous.

"Oh my god, what are you doing?!" I shrieked a little louder than I meant to. Was someone trying to sabotage my play?

The pounding and drilling stopped, and four pairs of eyes rocketed toward me.

One pair was a stormy gray and belonged to none other than Lachlan Adair. He stood up, wiped his hands on his work pants, and jogged over. "You're early, Director!"

"Lachlan, what is this?" The more I stared at it, the more familiar it seemed.

"It's a set. I built it for you." I had never seen him grin so broadly.

"Are you serious?" It was a scaffolding with three levels, built out of solid wood and stained a dark brown. "You...built this? Yourself?" There was also what looked like a judge's bench and a witness stand attached to the end of the first level on stage right.

He nodded. "Once you told me what you envisioned for the show, I started building it in my garage. Finished the last bit up in the shop here at work, and my work buddies helped me bring it over and assemble it. Hey, guys, come here a sec, will ya?" He pointed at the judge's bench. "That's detachable and can move to center stage for the courtroom scene." He gestured to the other side. "And over here is the jail cell for the first scene, also detachable."

Four men laid down their tools and joined us in front of the performance area, all wearing smiles on their faces and IU facility management uniforms on their bodies.

"This is Ben, Chuck, Will and Jeff," Lachlan introduced, and the four men gave a bow in unison.

"I don't even know what to say!" My eyes were welling with tears—no one had ever done anything so thoughtful for me before. I stepped over to examine the structure. "The craftsmanship is just stunning. How did… how did you know the dimensions and what would work for the show?"

"I measured everything, of course. I know it's gonna take the cast a little while to get accustomed to it, but I figured I'd be the one on it the most, and I've been planning this for a while, so I was keeping it in mind while I was learning my blocking. I've been thinking about the timing to climb the stairs and jump down or whatever the scene calls for."

"It's just…I…" I kept shaking my head, words eluding me. "I don't know how to thank you for this. This is incredible. No one is going to have a set like this for their shows. No one."

"You said the different levels would be symbolic," he reminded me of a conversation we'd shared what felt like ages ago now. "It seemed important to you. So I figured I'd build it."

The reality of it was making my mind spin with questions. "The wood must've cost a fortune! Please let me pay you back f—"

My protest died on my lips when he pressed a finger to them and shook his head. He smelled like sweat and sawdust, and I'd never seen him look so sexy. Okay, maybe not as sexy as he was in his kilt, but this was damn near close.

Before I could say anything else, the other members of the cast began to trickle into the theater. "Holy shit! What's this?" a few exclaimed as they stood gawking at the enormous structure.

It looked like something you'd see in a professional show. It actually reminded me of the set for *Hamilton*, but even that was only one level above the stage. This had two levels in the center section. I couldn't get over how incredible it was.

"Let us finish the assembly." Lachlan nodded to his coworkers. They all headed back over to pick up their tools where they'd left them before the introductions were made.

Kady, who played Ruth in the play, sauntered over to me, her eyes still glued to the set. "He made that for you?"

I nodded, still too flabbergasted to properly form words.

"Are you guys married in real life?" the nineteen-year-old pondered.

I shook my head.

"You're in love with each other though, right?"

I turned to meet her wide-eyed, inquisitive stare. I tried to hide my smile as I gave a little shrug.

"Yeah you are," was all she said in response.

"How was your last dress rehearsal?" Poe asked when I got home.

"It went well." I looked around. It seemed way too quiet in our house. "Where is everyone?"

"Cynda, Jason and Darth went out to meet up with two of Cynda's other friends who apparently just started dating. Aris and Noah are their names. She's so excited—she fixed them up." Poe laughed. "That woman—she is quite the matchmaker. She still can't top me introducing you to Lachlan though."

"Speaking of Lachlan, you're never going to believe what he did," I teased my girlfriend's curiosity.

I got the desired response: her classic eyebrow arch. "Tell me!" she demanded.

"He designed and built a set for the play—by hand! It's this enormous scaffolding, kinda like the one from *Hamilton*, only cooler, with two levels above the stage plus a courtroom piece and a jail cell. I told him when we first started rehearsals what I'd envisioned for a set if I could have one, and he nailed it. It's even curved to account for the sight lines of the audience on the sides. I am still trying to get over how much time and money it might have cost him."

"Wow." She walked to the kitchen and got out two wine glasses. "I have a roast in the crockpot. Should be ready soon."

I took the glass of wine she offered. "We need to talk about this, don't we?"

She looked up at me. "What do you mean?"

"Ever since we were at my parents' house on Sunday, and they were so obsessed with Lachlan coming to the wedding, you've been distant. I know things are going well with Delaney, and I'm happy for you. Are you," I choked down a sip of wine for some liquid courage to ask her what I was worried about, "are you thinking of breaking up with me now that I have Lachlan and you have Delaney?"

"What?" She sat down on the sofa. "Of course not! Why would you think that?"

"Because the way you react to me talking about him has changed. And you've become a lot more private with your feelings for Delaney. I just feel like something has shifted between us."

She took a long drink of wine and set the glass down on the coffee table. "I don't want to break up with you. It wouldn't be much of a polyamorous relationship if I dumped you just because you started dating someone else and so have I. Relationships shift and change when life changes, when different people come into your life and the dynamics change. There's nothing wrong with that."

"Are you saying you don't want to be primary partners anymore?" Putting words to my fears made my heart thunder in my chest.

"I never said that." She looked down at her nails for a second, chipping away at some old polish. "I never used the term 'primary' anyway."

"Well, it's been a while since you dated anyone as steadily as Delaney," I observed, "and I have never had anyone else. I just—I don't know what's changed between us, but I don't like it."

"It's not Lachlan," she insisted. She let out a breathy sigh and sat for a moment, like she needed to fortify herself to tell me what the real problem was. "It's your family."

"I know they suck," I retorted. "Trust me. But you knew going in what they were like. And I didn't hide you from them—"

"No, you just hide the true nature of our relationship,"

she fired back. When I started to argue, she held her hand up. "Do you ever intend to come out of the closet? Are you going to get married just so you can keep your inheritance?"

"What?! No! I would never—"

"But you might let them think there's a chance you will," she said. "In order to stay in their good graces."

I was silent. She wasn't wrong. And I felt a lot of guilt about that—but dealing with them was tricky. And I wasn't ready to be disowned. Even though I disagreed with their beliefs, their politics, their—well, most everything—for some reason, I still craved their acceptance, their approval—their love.

"Taking Lachlan to the wedding would go a long way in throwing them off the scent, wouldn't it?" she conjectured. It almost sounded like an accusation.

I ran my hands through my hair, wincing when my fingers caught on a tangle. "It would, but I won't take him if it's too upsetting to you. I love you, Poe, and I hate that this situation hurts you so much. I just—I don't want to ruin our chances of being able to move to New York."

"Moving to New York is your dream, not mine," she admitted.

My head whipped toward her. "What?! You've always wanted to live there! And it's near your family. Who is, admittedly, much cooler than mine."

She shook her head. "No, I wanted the picture you painted where you said it would be this progressive place where we could be together, be out as lovers and as polyamorous folks." She swallowed hard, and then her jaw tightened. "But I want that here. Not in New York."

"So what are you saying?" Tears burned at the corners

of my eyes as I tried to grasp a future so contrary to the one I thought we were working toward and dreaming of.

"I don't want to leave Delaney," she admitted, taking my hand into hers. "And you probably don't want to leave Lachlan either. I know you guys have really bonded, and I think that's amazing. I love that for you. He built you a set, Molly. He is in love with you. I have no doubt."

I shook my head, unable to believe her words. "No… he's never said that, Poe. It's just a fling. He's probably going to Scotland next semester for work, and he might not come home—"

The reasons he told me for being reticent to visit his family were adorable, but I was sure once he got there, and they saw what he'd made of himself, all the teasing of the past would be just that—in the past. And he might want to stay. Besides the fact that he couldn't stay over here indefinitely. Wouldn't his visa expire at some point?

I never thought of Lachlan as being a permanent fixture in my life.

Though thinking of losing him also threatened to rip my heart in two.

"What are you thinking?" Poe wondered, still holding my hand.

I bit my lip, trying to keep a tear from dripping down my cheek. "I don't know what to think. I just need to get through this play, Poe. This weekend is the single most important weekend of my entire career, and there's so much riding on it. I just—this is too much—"

She wrapped her arms around me and pulled me to her chest. "You're right. I shouldn't have brought all this up right now. When I heard about Lachlan's surprise set… well, I knew it had meaning. And we do need to have more conversations about your family, but it can wait. It can wait until the weekend is over. I still need to ask you one more thing though."

When I glanced up at her from my cradled position in her embrace, my tear won its fight to escape from my eye. It streaked down my cheek, leaving a cool trail in its wake. "What's that?"

"Do you mind if I bring Delaney to the play tomorrow night?" her voice was almost a whisper.

"Oh, of course you can." I smiled up at her.

She blinked, and a tear rolled down her cheek as well. "Are you sure? I don't want to make things worse."

"It won't," I promised. "I would love for her to see it. You know I support your relationship with her. I haven't gotten to know her that well yet, but she seems lovely. Jason and Cynda are coming tomorrow night too, you know. And that means probably Darth as well."

She smiled and nodded. "Yes, I figured we'd all sit together. That way you have a big cheering section, all of us rooting for you."

I pressed my lips to her cheek. "Thank you for that. Thank you for everything. We'll figure this out, darling. I know we will."

Her lips brushed against mine. "I know we will too."

eighteen

. . .

lachlan

I GAVE my closing speech as Hamish. The proverbial curtain fell, and a thunderous applause exploded, raining down on me like confetti as the rest of the cast joined Kady and me in the spotlight for our bows. When the clapping started to wane, I pointed to Molly in the first row of the audience with one hand while making a fist with the other and pressing it to my heart.

At this, the crowd sprang to its feet, whooping and hollering their appreciation for the skill and talent of the playwright/director. She stood, both hands to her mouth, kissing them and then gesturing back to us, her cast. More applause ensued.

The high I felt was indescribable. I couldn't think of a time I felt more energized or prouder of myself. And proud of her. We had accomplished so much in such a short span of time, and here we were. To the victors go the spoils, and our treasure was showered down upon us in the form of applause.

We all stepped off the stage to reunite with our family, our friends, our fans, and the first thing I did was take Molly into my arms.

"You were fucking brilliant," she said in my ear, her voice shooting straight to my cock.

This was not a good venue for an erection, but she had that effect on me. I kissed her cheek and replied in her ear, "Can't wait to get you back to my house and show you some more brilliance."

She grinned ear to ear, then grabbed my hand to take me to her cheerleading section. I recognized Poe, Cynda, Jason and Darth.

"This is Delaney, Poe's girlfriend," she introduced.

"Pleased to meet you." I extended my hand, and she smiled and shook it. She was pretty—not what I expected perhaps. It was really cool that Molly and her polycule could be so supportive of each other. I didn't know how I fit into all of it, but they were genuinely nice people.

"We're so fucking proud of you!" Poe exclaimed and swept Molly into her arms for a kiss.

I glanced around, trying to see if anyone noticed we'd both kissed her. No one seemed to be paying any attention to us.

Poe turned to me and gave me a playful punch on the arm. "You were great out there. I knew you would be. I'm thinking about moving to Hollywood to become a casting director," she joked.

"I think I was the biggest skeptic of all of us," I admitted, "but you knew what you were doing!"

We all laughed. Delaney executed a dramatic Victorian-era swoon, leaning back with her hand over her forehead like she might faint. "Your accent is just so dreamy. I could listen to you talk all day."

"Have to admit I thickened it up a bit for Hamish." I gave her a wink.

She shook her head, long blonde curls flying around her shoulders. "Oh, don't tell me that. I wanna believe you seduced the pants right off Molly with that gorgeous brogue!"

We all laughed again. Molly wrapped her arm around me. "He doesn't even need that accent when he has such a talented tongue."

Aye, everyone was loving this banter. It was different than joking around with my rugby lads, but still fun. I wanted to get Molly back to my place, though, so I needed to wrap this up.

"I'm glad you approve, beautiful." I leaned down and whispered in her ear, "Now let me take you home so I can use it on you."

Her skin flushed ever so slightly. I loved the fact that she was this progressive, sex-positive polyamorous bisexual lady, and yet her pale skin flushed so easily. I loved watching the pink bloom on her cheeks and upper chest.

"Well, we need to get going." Molly looked up at me with a smile, then addressed her friends again, "Thank you all for coming. It means so much to me. When this is over, we're going out, and the first round is on me, okay? Can't offer much more being a poor grad student and all."

"Is your advisor and your thesis committee here tonight?" Cynda glanced around at the few people who remained in the audience. Almost everyone had swarmed the actors on stage after our bows or already left the theater.

"No, my advisor is coming tomorrow, and so is my family. Then the rest of the committee on Sunday. So wish me luck!" she stated. "My advisor told me she has connections at a couple of theaters in Indy—so there may be scouts here tomorrow night too."

"Wow, that's so exciting!" Poe leaned in and pulled Molly into her arms again. She whispered something in her ear, and Molly laughed, but I didn't catch what she said.

I studied Delaney's face, and there wasn't a trace of jealousy. We said goodnight to everyone and headed backstage to grab our things.

I swung open the door and flipped on the lights in the green room. "I'm glad Poe dropped you off so you can ride with me."

The rest of the cast had cleared out, so I stripped out of my costume. I hung it neatly on some hangers and left it on a metal clothing rack on the far wall.

"Me too. Maybe we can grab something to eat on the way to your house? I couldn't eat before the show—my nerves—and now I'm starving."

"Depends on how good of a girl you plan on being once we get there." I shot her a mischievous grin.

"If it gets me something good to eat, I'll be the goodest girl ever!" she promised with a wink.

After Chinese takeout and showers, Molly and I finally made it to the bedroom. I'd taken Bonnie Skye out while Molly was in the shower, and my pup was so knackered, she passed right out in her wee bed. Darth was spending the night with Cynda and Jason, so we had the house to ourselves.

"Are you ready for me, lassie?" I asked as Molly came into the room wearing only a towel.

She sighed. "Your shower is heavenly. I think I need something like that at our house. Can you hook me up?"

"Aye, I'm pretty handy. Don't know if you've noticed." Chuckling, I lifted my hands in front of me and wiggled my fingers.

She swept over to my bed and dropped the towel, revealing her delectably curvy body, all flushed and steamy from her shower. "Do your worst," she offered herself up, flinging herself onto the mattress and striking a provocative pose.

Who could resist such an alluring invitation? I'd slipped on a pair of gray sweats and a loose t-shirt to take Bonnie out, so I ripped the shirt off and flung it to the side. I looked down to where the waistband of the sweats rode low on my hips, my growing bulge straining against the fabric.

She licked her lips. "Fuck, those sweatpants look absolutely mouthwatering on you, but I think I'm ready for the big reveal." She rubbed her hands together, and I stood, slowly rotating my hips. "Fuck, don't tease me! Lose the pants, Lach!"

"Lach, huh?"

"Sir?" She batted her eyelashes at me.

"That's more like it." I climbed onto the bed, straddling her. "I'll take them off when I'm ready."

She pouted, but I hooked her chin with my index finger and forced her eyes to mine. "Are you doing to be a good girl, or do we need to start off with a punishment?"

She shook her head and bit her lip to suppress a smile. "I'll be good."

"I know you can give direction, but can you take it as

well? I did everything you asked of me on stage as Hamish tonight, so now it's your turn to do everything I ask of you. Is that clear?"

"Yes, sir."

"Very good. We're going to start simply." I reached in my trousers and withdrew my cock, long, hard and ready for her mouth. I moved up her body and tapped the tip to her lips. "Now, suck."

She looked up at me, her green eyes burning right through mine as she complied with my command. Her tongue darted out to taste me, and her lashes fluttered as she savored the drop of my essence that dripped onto her lip. Then her mouth parted, and she took the head of my cock inside, wrapping her lips around it and running her tongue around the ridge underneath as my eyes rolled back in my head.

"That's it, lassie. Take a little more now."

I leaned forward, placing one of my hands under her head to lift her toward me, guiding her up and down on my shaft as my other hand gripped the headboard for balance. I continued to feed her, letting her slurp me deep inside and then withdraw before I thrust back down again, so deep she gagged a little. Seeing her cheeks hollow and her eyes tear up as she attempted to get as much of me down her throat as she could was such a fucking turn-on, I could have exploded right then and there.

But I was saving myself tonight.

"Good girl," I praised as I slid down her body. She looked a little disappointed at first that I'd taken her toy away, but she was soon gasping in a sharp breath when my mouth and teeth found her nipples and began to work them both over. I loved how responsive they were, how they hardened instantly under my tongue. I nibbled and chewed until she was bucking her hips and begging for relief.

"Do you need to come, lassie?"

"Yes, sir," she rasped. "Please?"

"Let's see…" I slid down further until my body was at the very end of the mattress, with me on my knees and my face in between her thighs. "Spread them for me, baby," I directed, and she moaned as I swiped a finger from her clit all the way to her asshole. "You're ready for me to take you here tonight." It was a statement, not a question.

"Yes, sir," she agreed, her back arching at the contact.

The thought of fucking her ass made me so fucking hard, I ached. But I was determined to make her come first. I licked her labia, sucking them into my mouth and making her squirm beneath me before I finally attended to her clit, which elicited a sharp gasp from her mouth. While my tongue twirled in circles around it, intermittently sucking it into my mouth, my finger stroked down to her back hole, just teasing it lightly. When I was fairly certain she was about to come unglued, I stopped.

"What the fuck?!" She bolted upright and glared down at me, fire in her eyes.

"Hold on, I need to get some lube."

"Hold on?! Hold on?! What kind of sadistic mother-fucker are you?" she demanded as I tried to suppress my laughter. After pulling a bottle of lube from the drawer beside my bed, I squirted a few drops on my finger.

"Trust the process," I told her, which awarded me a smirk. That was a phrase she uttered all the time while directing our play, especially when she made us do various exercises to get the emotion or timing right in a scene.

I slowly worked up to what I had been doing before I

rudely and heartlessly stopped. Her hips were writhing in rhythm with my finger buried deep inside her pussy until I withdrew it, spreading her juices and the lube to her puckered hole. One fingertip in—so tight, it was hard to imagine my cock would ever fit.

When I made it to my first knuckle, she was screaming as an orgasm ripped through her like a tidal wave, her whole body jerking off the bed. Her asshole spasmed so hard, I thought it might squeeze off my finger. Damn!

As she rode the crest and came back down to earth, I applied more lube to my finger and also to my other hand so I could stroke my cock while I prepared her for me. As soon as she was ready to go again, I lowered my mouth to her swollen folds and clit and gradually began to coax her body into another frenzied orgasm.

This time, she reached down and threaded her fingers through my hair, holding me in place so she could fuck my face, her hips rhythmically driving her pussy with increasing intensity. By the time she came down from her climax, I had managed to get two fingers inside her.

She was ready for me.

I met her gaze, her heaving chest and hooded lids telling me she was satiated. "Are you going to fuck my ass?" she questioned, barely getting the words out between pants as her body fought for equilibrium.

"Yes, lassie." I rose to my knees, showing off my throbbing cock as it slipped in and out of my fist, the head so engorged, it was nearly purple. I had a condom ready to go and took my time unrolling it so she could see how fucking hard she made me. "I will try not to hurt you. Tell me if I need to stop."

"Do you think you can?" She was breathing more

normally now, evidently starting to get her senses about her.

"Yes..." was the simplest answer I could give, then I added, "I can, but I won't want to."

"I want to make you feel as good as you've made me feel tonight." She bit her lip and looked at me with desire shining in her eyes.

"You will," was my promise.

I pressed the tip against her entrance, and her eyes clenched shut. "Relax, lassie. This will never work if you can't relax."

"I know..." her soft voice drifted on the air. "I'm trying."

She fisted the sheets as I pushed forward a little more. Fuck, her ring of muscles was so tight, it almost hurt my cock, but my balls were aching with my need for release, so I pushed a little harder, a little deeper. "That's a good girl. Just like that...relax and let go. It's gonna feel so good when I get going. I promise you."

She let out a sharp scream as my head fully breached her opening. "That's the worst of it," I assured her. "Ah... fuck...lassie...oh, god, yeh feel so fuckin' good..."

"All the way," she gasped, "I want you all the way inside me. Don't stop."

With that encouragement, I slid in, inch by inch, letting her adjust as I went. Then I held myself there, buried to the hilt in her ass as her lips parted, her eyes clenched tightly again as she breathed and assimilated to the feel of my thick cock stretching her.

"Fuck me, Lachlan," she urged, her eyes opening and locking onto mine. "Please, I wanna make you come."

I closed my eyes and tightened my grip on her legs as I made a few slow pumps inside her. Her eyes rolled back in her head as pleasure began to override the pain. The pressure of each thrust shot through me from my balls to my extremities as I struggled to avoid falling over the edge. I wanted to make this last—hopefully make her come again.

I found my stride and picked up speed. She reached down and clasped both hands around my upper arms, squeezing my biceps. "I want to turn over so you can really fuck me hard."

"Your wish is my command." I pulled out and, in one swift motion, flipped her over onto her knees.

The break gave me a little time to calm myself down, which I extended by teasing her hole with the tip, sliding it in and then out. She whimpered, "Please…Lachlan," and reached between her legs to rub her clit.

Her desperate moans would be my undoing as I slid back in to the hilt. Fingers buried in her fleshy hips, I sped up my pace, slamming into her until I could take no more.

My climax tore through me, a primal roar bellowing from deep in my lungs as my cum rocketed up my shaft. It was all I could do to hold on and let the ecstasy rock through me, stealing my vision, my breath, and every last thought in my mind.

After I cleaned us up, I gathered her into my arms. Her eyes closed as she snuggled into my embrace. I hadn't turned off my bedside lamp yet, so I could still see the satiated smile on her face as she just relaxed and breathed.

I thought she may have fallen asleep when I whispered, "I am still not sure how I fit into all the poly stuff, but I am sure of one thing. I've fallen for you, Molly Rose. I've fallen hard." I pressed a kiss to her cheek. "I love you."

Her eyes still closed, she snuggled even closer as she whispered back, "I love you too."

nineteen

. . .

molly

I HAD PACED from one end of the green room to the other and back again about a hundred times. I had to stop. I would make the entire cast nervous. I couldn't seem to force my feet to halt their motion, so Lachlan grabbed my wrist, jerking me back with such force that I wound up on his lap.

Not a bad place to land, mind you.

"You're gonna wear a trench in the carpet if you keep pacing like that," he warned. His knee bounced up and down a few times. "Everything went brilliantly last night. What has you so on edge tonight?"

I took a deep breath and tried to calm my racing heart. "For one, my parents, my sister and her fiancé are here. Two, there are two directors here—one from a theater in Indianapolis, and the other from one in Fort Wayne. Lachlan, there's a lot riding on tonight's performance. My advisor just texted me to break a leg."

"Well, that's all good stuff," Lachlan assured me as the

rest of the cast started to filter in. They didn't look very pumped up, let alone ready to deliver the performance of their lives.

I stood up and stretched my arms above my head. "C'mon, guys, we're gonna do some warm-ups. Let's get our blood flowing. We need to knock 'em dead tonight."

There was a low rumbling of half-hearted assent.

"I mean it. Everyone front and center, now!" I brought out my teacher voice. I didn't use it much, but I'd perfected it during the five or six years I taught high school English, and boy did it come in handy when I wanted to command people's attention.

Lachlan stood up too, took a deep breath and puffed out his chest. He was already in costume—his prison jumpsuit to start. I'd somehow found chambray coveralls in his size in the costume loft. His makeup was done too. He was ready to go—and no black eye from his rugby game today because he missed it so he wouldn't be too worn out for this show.

Between that and building the set for me, I knew his feelings for me must be strong. Thinking about that made me so warm and tingly inside. *Okay, I can do this*, I told myself. *I have too much riding on this to fail now.*

"Last night was great, guys, but tonight is even more important. My parents are in the audience, for one thing. And, for another, there are some directors—i.e. talent scouts—in the audience from a couple big theaters in Indianapolis and Fort Wayne. So let's commit to wowing them right now, okay?"

Everyone clapped and shouted their agreement. That was more like it.

We stretched. We did some vocal warmups. And then it was time. "Places, everyone!"

I had to be the director, the stage manager, the prop master, the costume designer—I was doing everything but running light and sound. Fortunately, I had help for those things. I needed to take a moment to just breathe before I had to be wheeled out of this theater in a straitjacket.

Lachan pulled me aside right before I left to find my seat. "We're gonna do great, lassie. Don't you worry your pretty little head." He pressed a kiss to my forehead. "See you after the show."

lachlan

The curtain call—though there was no real curtain—was still underway when I finally broke character and looked out into the audience. Front and center, Molly was beaming, clapping and shouting at us, her cast. I gestured to her so everyone could express their congratulations, and she moved her hand to her heart, soaking in the adulation. I loved seeing her like that—her eyes shining and the brightest smile on her face.

After we began to disperse, a woman in a long black dress left her seat in the front row and walked right up to me. "Great job up there. I'm Allison Finley." She extended her hand to greet me.

"Hi, Allison, Lachlan Adair," I introduced myself. "Thank you for coming to the show."

"I'm the creative director at the Central Indiana Playhouse in Indianapolis. Is it true this is your first show ever? No other acting experience?"

I chuckled. "Aye, you heard correctly. I work in facility maintenance at the biology building here on campus."

"Very impressive! And I understand you designed and built the set yourself?" Her dark eyes were flashing with admiration as she leaned closer to me so I could hear her above the noise of the crowd.

I glanced over to see that Molly was talking with her sister, her soon-to-be brother-in-law and two other people I assumed were her parents. Then another woman in a black skirt and pink sweater interrupted. I wondered who she was.

Alison nudged me, and when I looked back at her, she was holding a business card out for me to take. "I'm sorry if I got you at a bad time, Mr. Adair, but I just wanted to pick your brain about the set for a moment."

"I'm sorry," I gestured around the theater, "just a little distracted. Lot going on tonight. Yes, I designed and built the set."

"I'm very impressed with the angles you used to preserve the sightlines. And you've never taken a design course?"

I shook my head. "No, no, just have a love of building things, that's all."

"Give me a call if you're ever in downtown Indy and would like to grab a cup of coffee sometime," she said. "Again, great job tonight. Very impressive performance." She patted me on the shoulder and went over to join Molly and the woman in the pink sweater. Molly's family must have left. They weren't with her any longer.

Poe had struck up a conversation with Kady on the other side of the theater. I was about to head over to say hello when I felt a tap on my arm. I turned around to see Molly's sister Meredith standing there with a smile that looked like it ran in the family.

"Hi, Lanny, great job tonight! I wanted to make sure you got to meet my parents." She gestured to the couple, who appeared to be in their fifties, standing beside her.

"Molly's talking to some professional theater folks, and we were just getting ready to leave. But I didn't want to go without introducing you to my mom and dad. You'll see them again at the wedding next weekend!"

"Oh, hello. Lachlan Adair." I extended my hand to shake first her mom's hand, and then her dad's. "Hello again, Eli." I shook Meredith's fiancé's hand as well.

"I'm Tom Rose, and this is my wife, Jane," her father introduced himself. He was a tall, wiry man with graying hair and glasses. His wife was built like Molly, but she had short salt-and-pepper hair.

"We're so thrilled you're coming to the wedding!" Jane gushed. "You did an amazing job in the play. We're so excited that you and Molly met." She looked like she was about to burst, she was so animated. I now saw where Molly got her mannerisms from.

"I'm excited too," I assured them, though I didn't know we had decided for sure that I was going and not Poe.

Speaking of whom… I looked up and caught Poe's eye. She noticed me talking to Mr. and Mrs. Rose, her face scrunched up, and then she bolted offstage, vanishing within seconds.

"It was great to meet you both," I said. "I have to run. I'm so sorry. See you next weekend."

I took off running after Poe, behind the set and through the doors to backstage. Once I was in the bowels of the theater building, I wasn't sure which way she went. I checked the green room, but she wasn't there. There was a costume shop on this level and a scene shop, but both those doors would be locked.

The restrooms! I jogged down the hall and threw open the women's restroom door. "Poe? Poe, are you in here?"

No answer.

I checked the men's restroom too, just in case. As I was walking out, I heard someone calling my name down the hall. I jogged back toward the green room to find Molly standing there.

"What's wrong?"

I huffed, still out of breath, "Poe ran out when she saw me talking to your parents and sister."

She sighed. "Fuck. I better go find her. Go on home. I'll text you later."

It was only ten-thirty when I climbed into my truck. My body was full of adrenaline, and my mind was stuffed with rambling thoughts. I texted Sam to ask him where he and the other lads were. Maybe they were still partying after our match today.

We're at The Irish Lion, he texted back. *We lost today without you. Misery loves company. Get your ass over here.*

I pulled out of the car park and headed downtown. Maybe a few drinks with the lads would get this bad taste out of my mouth.

molly

"Poe?" I jiggled the bathroom door handle. "Are you in here?"

The water stopped running, and the lock disengaged. Then the door handle turned. "I'm sorry. I'm just struggling with this right now."

"Come on, let's talk." I reached out to take her hand.

"Everyone went out to a late movie, so they won't be home for a while. We can talk in the living room."

She sighed and nodded, wiping a tear from her cheek before following me. She sank into the couch cushions and buried her head in her hands, her long hair falling around her like a curtain. "I suck," she mumbled. "I shouldn't be having this much trouble with this."

I sat down next to her and put my hand on her knee. "It's okay to feel whatever you feel, Poe. Don't apologize for being human and having feelings."

She looked up at me, her eyes puffy and swollen. "I don't have a problem with you and Lachlan. But I understand why you want to take him to the wedding and not me."

"It's not that I want to take him and not you," I said without hesitation. "I would take both of you if I could! Actually, that would be the ideal solution, but my family would freak the fuck out. We all know this! I'm surprised I didn't get a lecture right there in the theater about the foul language in the play. My mother forgot to wear her pearls, so she couldn't spend the evening clutching them."

That garnered a little giggle from my girlfriend, whose lips cracked a smile. She took in a deep, shuddering breath. "Just take him. I'll get over it. I promise."

I chose to ignore her statement for now. She had a tendency to play the martyr sometimes, and she was highly emotional at the moment. At this point, I was probably going to attend my sister's wedding alone—which was fine with me and seemed like the best way to avoid hurting Poe's feelings or making Lachlan feel like he was on display. My mother might start planning a wedding for him and me if he went as my plus-one.

"I wanted to tell you about the conversation I had after

the show. I came to find you, but you had already left." I patted her knee again.

"I ran out when I saw your family schmoozing with Lachlan. I'm sorry about that—I overreacted. So what did they say? That you're brilliant and going to be a famous playwright someday?"

I laughed. "I spoke with the two directors from the theaters in Indy and Fort Wayne. Both were interested in bringing *Scot Free* to their stages—possibly in the spring."

Her jaw dropped open a little, and she just stared at me for a moment. "Are you serious?"

I chuckled. "Yes. Obviously Indianapolis is a lot closer than Fort Wayne, but it is a hike. I might have to consider staying there overnight on occasion, but I wouldn't be directing. I'd license them the rights to produce it. I know the Central Indiana Playhouse has had original plays optioned for off-Broadway productions. I might be able to do this from here, is what I'm saying. Not from New York. What do you say?"

"I think that would be amazing!" She gave a genuine smile now. "It doesn't solve the issue with your family, but—"

"Well, if I was generating my own income and didn't have to rely on the trust fund, that would help a lot," I reminded her.

She squeezed my hand. "Right."

"There's something else I want to tell you." I turned to face her, making sure I had her full attention.

"What's that?"

"Last night, Lachlan told me he was still unsure about how the poly thing was going to work, but that he's in love with me." I couldn't say the words without smiling.

"Wow, babe! That's amazing!" She leaned in and

wrapped her arms around me. "I'm so happy for you guys."

"Yay! It means a lot to me to hear you say that." I ran my fingers through her hair. "How is it going for you and Delaney in that department?"

She pulled back, and a huge grin spread across her face. "I haven't told her yet...but I'm thinking maybe tomorrow. I know you have the show, so I was thinking of spending the day with her."

"That sounds great, sweetheart. I'm happy for you too."

twenty

. . .

lachlan

I DRAGGED my hungover arse out of bed around ten o'clock, and as soon as the time registered in my brain, I realized I needed to get moving if I was going to make my makeup call for our two o'clock matinee. This was our final performance, and it was the most important one. The committee that would decide if Molly's production met the standards required for her to complete the master's program would be in attendance. No pressure.

After starting the coffee, I put Bonnie on her lead and took her out to do her business. The crisp fall air made goosebumps spike all over my body as I chastised myself for not putting on something warmer.

Then a car pulled into the driveway, deepening my regret for wearing so little to walk the dog. At first, I thought it was Darth coming home from a night with his girlfriend—and boyfriend? I didn't really know how to label their relationship. As I told Molly the other night, I was still tackling how I felt about this polyamory thing.

But it wasn't Darth.

"Hey, you wanna put some pants on or what?" came Poe's voice from her rolled-down window.

What was she doing here?

"Just a sec," I grumbled, "trying to get my dog to take a dump, *ye ken*?"

She rolled her eyes and climbed out of her car, shivering as she stood there in a hoodie and yoga pants. As soon as Bonnie was done, they both followed me inside. I still didn't understand why she was here.

"Do you want some coffee?" I asked as I hung Bonnie's lead up by the door. When I headed back into the kitchen, Poe followed on my heels just like my dog usually did. "Is something wrong? Is Molly okay?"

She settled in on a stool across from me as I stood at the counter pouring coffee. "I wanted to have a chat with you —metamour to metamour."

"Meta-what?" I blinked a few times. "Do you want coffee or not?"

She sighed. "No coffee. A metamour is your partner's partner—if they aren't your partner too, they are your metamour. Didn't Cynda explain that the other night when you were over?"

"Yeah, sorry, guess it didn't register." This poly lingo was confusing. "You were upset last night and ran out. I tried to track you down before you left—"

She held up a hand. "I'm sorry about that. I..." She shook out her hands and shoulders like she needed to clear her nerves. Was she scared to talk to me?

This felt weird and wrong. "Does Molly know you're here?"

"No," she answered, "but she and I talked last night.

About you, about her sister's wedding, and about us moving to New York—"

"She doesn't know you're here?" Maybe I needed more coffee. My head was pounding, and Bonnie was begging for her breakfast. I took as big of a gulp as I could stand—damn, it was hot.

She laced her fingers together and placed them on the countertop. "It's okay. Like I said, we're talking metamour to metamour. There's nothing wrong with that."

"Well, I'm not very comfortable with it." I crossed my arms over my chest.

Bonnie let out a sharp bark and bolted to the window that looked out on the driveway. That engine rumble was familiar—this time it was Darth. Bonnie wasn't going to stop barking until he came inside, so I held up a finger to stop Poe from talking, then I filled Bonnie's food bowl. This conversation was giving me even more of a headache than the hangover.

"Hey." He greeted us curtly and gave Bonnie a single pat on her head, which was his custom, and she dug into her breakfast. Next thing I knew, he was in the kitchen pulling out eggs, cheese, and veggies.

"So, as I said," Poe continued, "Molly and I talked last night, and we decided you should go with her to the wedding—even though I really wanted to go, and I am kind of hurt that she would take you instead."

"Wait." I processed what she just said, and, *och*, that headache was really starting to pound at my temples. Her voice—her whole presence—was grating on my nerves. I didn't feel right talking about Molly when she wasn't here.

"Wait, what?" She blinked a few times, seeming offended I'd interrupted her.

"You can go to the wedding with her, then, if you

wanna go so bad," I said. "I don't give a fuck about going to a wedding. Her parents and sister seem nice enough, but if it's hurting your feelings, then you go. Whatever."

She shook her head. "You don't understand. Didn't Molly tell you about her family?"

"About them being religious freaks? Aye."

"The reason I can't go with her is that they don't know she and I are dating," she explained. "She's in the closet. They don't know she's bi, and they don't know she's poly. If she takes you, then she can pass for straight and make them happy."

"What, you're saying she's using me to get on their good side?" I slammed my empty coffee mug down on the counter and immediately refilled it.

"Not exactly, but she does have to be careful to stay on their good side, or they might take away her trust fund. She inherited money from her grandfather and—"

I held up my hand again, my frustration making my accent thicken. "*Ah dinnae wan' tae talk aboot this. Ah willnae go tae the weddin'.*"

"No, I'm saying you should go with her," she insisted, clearly feeling just as frustrated as I was. "I just wanted you to know I'm upset about it, but it's not your fault, and…well, I'll get over it eventually, but I—"

I didn't like this. It seemed unnecessarily complicated. I wasn't ready for this kind of drama. If this was what polyamory was, I didn't want any part of it.

I swallowed hard and tried to speak clearly: "Look, I'm tired, I'm hungover, and I need to get ready for my show."

Not to mention the fact that Darth is still three feet away from me, making a particularly smelly omelet while I'm arguing with my girlfriend's girlfriend. I felt like I'd just stepped into Bizarro World.

"You don't need to get all bent out of shape," Poe snarked at me. "I came over here to talk to you so we could get to know each other, so we could get on the same page. If we're both going to be in love with Molly, then we need to communicate and figure out a way to share our love so we're all happy and fulfilled."

"You don't seem to be getting this right now," I seethed, completely fed up by this point. Now I'd gone from Scottish slang to full-on British Crown-quality enunciation: "I don't want to be part of this. I like things simple. I like things easy. Go to the wedding with Molly or don't. I'm not going to be the one who stands in the way of you getting to do things with her and her family. I'm not going to be the stand-in boyfriend who's presentable to her Mum and Dad, when you're getting left out in the cold. I just don't want to be part of that. It's not fair to anyone."

She stared at me, anger flaring in her hazel eyes. "So, what, are you breaking up with her then?"

I'd fucking had it with this childish shit. "Yeah, I guess so. Why? Yeh gonna run off and tell her like we're kids in school again?"

Poe jumped off the barstool and began marching toward the door. Before she flung it open, she had some parting words for me: "No. You'll have to grow a pair and tell her yourself."

molly

When I woke up, everyone was gone: Poe, Cynda, Jason, and Darth. Okay, not Sagan. Sagan was whining in the doorway to the kitchen like everyone had abandoned him, and he'd never been fed a day in his life.

So, the first thing I did was feed the cat.

Next, I scoured the house for any notes left for me that might indicate where everyone had gotten off to. Then I checked my phone for messages. Nada. Nothing. Zilch.

Finally, I looked at the clock and realized how late it was. Holy shit, did I ever sleep! I needed to get moving so I could get to the theater for the matinee on time. As I was running water for my shower, I texted Poe.

> Me: Hey, you left early! I guess you're spending the day with Delaney? Have fun. See you tonight.

Then I texted Lachlan.

> Me: Morning, sleepyhead! Sorry I didn't get a chance to text you last night when I got home. Poe was really upset about my parents and sister talking to you and pressuring you to go to the wedding with me. It's a big mess. But we'll work it out. We have a show to get through first, right?! See you soon!

After showering and getting ready to leave for the theater, I still hadn't received replies from either of them. I tried calling Lachlan to make sure he was awake and ready for the show, but he didn't answer. He was probably in the shower or outside with his sweet fur baby. No biggie.

I was starting to feel alone, and I never felt that way in this crazy house with people coming and going all the time. So, I texted Cynda while I waited for my food to heat up in the microwave.

> Me: Hey, lady! What are you guys up to today? Is Darth with you?

Reliable, loyal Cynda texted me back right away.

> Cynda: Jason and I went out for brunch. Darth went home this morning.

> Me: Oh, okay. Hey, do they have a landline over there? I haven't heard from Lachlan this morning, and I wanted make sure he knows what time to be at the theater.

> Cynda: No landline, but I can give you Darth's number if Lachlan isn't answering.

> Me: Could you? He's probably in the shower or out with his dog.

> Cynda: 812-555-3974. Good luck, sweetie.

Was that *good luck dealing with Lachlan,* or *good luck dealing with Darth*? Honestly, I probably needed a little luck to deal with either one of them.

To cover my bases, I decided to call Darth. It was time for me to leave for the theater, and I was starting worry that I hadn't heard back from my sexy Scotsman.

"Hello?"

"Darth, hi, this is Molly." I tried to make my voice sound as warm and pleasant as possible.

"Who?"

For fuck's sake. Do not have time for this right now. "Molly who lives with Cynda and Jason, and I'm dating your roommate."

"Oh, right." And then silence.

He was just fucking with me, wasn't he?

I swallowed hard. "Is Lachlan still there?"

"Who?"

I huffed out a breath but tried to keep my tone light. "Um, your roommate? Lanny?" That was what Darth and his other buddies called him.

"Oh, I don't know," came his super-helpful answer.

My head was beginning to throb. "What do you mean, you don't know?"

"I haven't seen him since he and Poe were fighting this morning," Darth elaborated. Sort of.

"What?" Now it was my turn to pose one-word questions.

"Poe—that's your girlfriend, right?"

"Yes, but—"

He cut me off, "She was here this morning. But she was mad and slammed the door when she left. It hurt my ears. I was making an omelet, but I wasn't hungry after hearing her scream. So now my day is ruined, and I'm going back to bed."

I ignored the part about the omelet. "What do you mean? What was she screaming about?"

"I don't know. I wasn't eavesdropping. I was just trying to make an omelet," he insisted.

My stomach dropped down to my knees. Why was Poe there? She didn't tell me she was going to talk to Lachlan. Why would she meddle in our relationship?

"You don't know if Lachlan—I mean Lanny—is there?"

"His truck is gone," Darth reported. It sounded like he'd walked to the living room to look out the window.

Well, that is a good sign, right? He was probably on his way to the theater. Speaking of which, I was going to be late if I didn't hurry up and get out of here.

"Okay, well, thanks for your help, Darth."

"Yep."

"Okay, goodbye."

He didn't say anything else. He just hung up. He was such a strange guy. I wondered what Cynda saw in him, but it was none of my business.

By the time I made it across town to the auditorium on campus, I was running late. I wanted to ask Poe what she was doing at Lachlan's house this morning, but I didn't want to interrupt her date with Delaney. And when I stepped into the green room and saw the scowl on Lachlan's face, I decided I'd have to talk to him later, after the show.

I went through warmups with everyone and thanked them again for all their hard work. "This is our last performance, guys, and this production has surpassed even my wildest dreams. I'll find out next week what my thesis committee thought and whether or not I will receive my MFA, but I am proud of everything we have achieved together. I have a good feeling. We just need to wow the audience for one more show—my committee members are out there today and will be taking notes. I have a little something for each of you after curtain call, so I'm going to leave all of these here." I held up a thick stack of white envelopes that contained thank-you cards and gift cards.

"Break a leg, guys!" I encouraged everyone before I left to join the audience. I stood there for a moment, waiting to see if Lachlan was going to speak to me, but he was in the middle of a conversation with Gabe, who played Tony, Lachlan's cellmate, in the show.

I would have to talk to him later. A bad feeling was gnawing at me in the pit of my stomach, and I hoped I could make it through the show without losing my mind.

We were three for three on standing O's.

I couldn't complain about that. My personal issues with Lachlan and Poe were temporarily forgotten as I basked in the thrill of being finished. I'd been working toward this master's degree for two years now. I'd left my teaching job to pursue this—taking a real leap of faith. I'd used money from my inheritance to finance the degree and sustain myself, all a huge risk.

I was standing on the precipice of all my dreams coming true.

Before I could talk to anyone in the cast, my advisor and other committee members surrounded me, all with beaming smiles on their faces.

"Well, done, Molly!" Bernie Vick congratulated me, patting me on the back.

"One of the best MFA student plays I've ever seen," Gloria Headley praised.

"I wouldn't be surprised if one of the directors who was here last night wants to produce it," Kat, my advisor, shared with me and her colleagues.

I was thrilled to receive such glowing accolades for my hard work, but the reality of my situation with Lachlan was starting to set in. "Excuse me, I just need to go speak with my cast members before they all leave," I told them.

"Of course, by all means." Kat patted me on the back, a proud smile on her face. "We'll see you for our meeting next week! Enjoy the rest of your day."

I headed toward the stage, where my actors were starting to disperse. Lachlan was talking to Kady, and as soon as I aimed in their direction, he disappeared through the black divider to the backstage area. Shit.

I crossed the stage, but I was stopped every few feet by cast members who wanted to chat about the show. A couple asked me to be references for acting jobs or grad school applications. By the time I made it backstage, I couldn't find Lachlan anywhere.

I pulled out my phone and sent him a text.

> Me: Hey, where'd you go? I was hoping we could chat.

He answered a few minutes later.

> Lachlan: Thank you for the opportunity to perform in your play. I really enjoyed it much more than I expected to. I will always remember our time together fondly.

My heart sank when I read his words. Was he breaking up with me? Who the fuck does that over text?

I had to find Poe and get some answers.

twenty-one

· · ·

lachlan

SUNDAY AFTER THE PLAY, I got a text from one of my rugby mates. I'd given him a ride home after we hung out the night before at The Irish Lion. He said he left his wallet in my truck and obviously needed it back ASAP, so I offered to meet him in town so he could pick it up.

> Kev from Rugby: You hungry? I was thinking about dinner at the Trojan Horse.
>
> Me: Yeah, I could go for a gyro. See you there in fifteen?
>
> Kev from Rugby: Sure.

The Trojan Horse in downtown Bloomington was one of my favorite restaurants. I pulled open the heavy wood door, and the aroma of Greek spices hit my nostrils. It was almost enough to make me forget that the play, Molly, and everything to do with it was over.

Almost.

"Hey," I greeted Kev who was in one of the first booths. I slid in and grabbed a menu.

"Hope you brought my wallet in, 'cause I'm gonna need it to pay." Kevin was one of the younger guys on the team, in his mid-twenties, and I was pretty sure he worked as a bartender at Kilroy's on Kirkwood.

I smacked it down on the table. "Here ya go."

"Thanks." He rifled through it as if checking whether his cash was still there. "Just teasin' ya. I trust you."

I chuckled just as the server stopped at our table to take our drink orders. When he left, I returned my attention to my mate. "Man, last night… I had a headache when I woke up this morning, and I didn't even drink that much."

"You didn't have much at all compared to me. Which is why you could drive home, and I couldn't." Kevin laughed. "I was surprised you came out. I thought you had plans since you weren't at the match yesterday."

"I was in a play," I admitted. "Finished up today, so I won't miss the last game of the season next weekend."

"That's good to hear," Kevin said. "Hey, is that the play your girlfriend wrote? I met her at Burke's party last weekend. She was telling me a little about it."

"Yeah, Molly wrote it," I answered. "She's not my girlfriend though."

"She's not?" He shrugged. "I could have sworn I saw you guys making out on the porch during the party. Love the pink hair. She's cute."

I sighed. I was really hoping no one saw that—especially since no one razzed me about it last night. As long as they didn't see how we defiled Burke's tractor, I supposed it was okay.

"Yeah, we hooked up, but she's not my girlfriend." After all, she had her own girlfriend.

"Hmm. Do you have her number? Maybe I could ask her out? She might be a few years older than me, but I've always had a thing for older women." He grinned as the server brought us our beers.

"I'm not giving you her number." I rolled my eyes at this dumb kid's audacity.

"Well, fuck, it sounds like you have a thing for her," he called me on it.

"She's cool and all, but she's bi and poly and has a girlfriend already," I shared.

His eyes bugged out. "What? Bi and has a girlfriend? That's fucking hot, dude. Threesome time!"

Fucking idiot. "Actually not how it works at all. Like I said, she's poly. She doesn't just fuck around, ya bawbag."

"What does that mean exactly? Poly?" he clarified.

I assumed he got the meaning of "bawbag" from context clues. "Poly, like in more than one relationship at a time."

"Oh, fuck that." He took a long pull off his beer. "I don't want to share my lady with nobody."

I rolled my eyes. Before I could say anything else, four familiar faces stepped foot inside the restaurant. It was Sam and his girlfriend, Kate, and Steve and his girlfriend, Ava.

"Hey, guys!" Kevin greeted them. "Guess everyone had the same idea tonight."

"Hey, Lanny, Kev. What's up?" Sam asked. The two women waved then walked past, giggling as they slid into a booth a little farther down.

"Lanny here was just telling me that pink-haired chick he nailed at the party is bi and poly," Kevin reported like he was a fucking news anchor or something.

"Bi? That's hot," Steve said. "What's poly mean?"

"Apparently it means sharing her with other people," Kevin paraphrased the definition I'd given.

"Oh, fuck no. Is she like one of those swinger chicks?" Sam asked.

I scrubbed a hand down my face. Why the fuck did I mention this to anyone? "She has a girlfriend, but they're also involved with other people," I shared—not sure why I was bothering, though. "Like independently of each other."

"Oh, got it," Sam said. "Yeah, I don't think I could ever do that. I can barely deal with one woman!"

"You certainly couldn't keep two satisfied in bed!" Kevin teased him.

Thankfully, our server came with our appetizers, and the two lads went to join their lassies.

Yeah, I could see that not too many people were cut out for the poly life.

I guess I was just another one of them.

I slept like shit Sunday night. Tossing and turning. All I could think was, a few nights ago, Molly was in that bed with me. And I told her I'd fallen in love with her.

That part was one hundred percent true. I just… I hadn't fully wrapped my head around the poly thing. I didn't know how it would work. Hearing all my friends tell me they could never get involved in that sort of relationship helped solidify that it wasn't for me.

Monday when I got to work, there was an email from my boss asking me to come to his office immediately. My heart pounded as I made my way to the facilities management office. Getting called to the boss's office was never fun—though I hoped it was something positive like what happened last time.

His admin assistant wasn't in yet, so I stopped right outside his office door and gave a little knock to the frame. "Hi, Boss, what can I do for you?"

"Hey, Lan, come on in. Have a seat." He gestured to the chair across from his desk. "Did you have a good weekend?"

"Yes, sir, thank you." I rested my ankle on top of my knee and laced my fingers together, waiting expectantly to hear what he had to say.

"We haven't gotten an answer from you yet about the research trip to Scotland." His tone was neutral, but I still felt like I needed to apologize. I still had two days till our agreed-upon deadline.

I hadn't given a firm answer because I was waiting—even if it was subconsciously—to see what happened with Molly after the play was over. I had been thinking about it ever since she and I had the conversation about my family and how they bullied me growing up. She encouraged me to give them another chance, insisting they would be proud of me and wouldn't think of me as a scrawny little kid anymore.

But I hadn't committed to going because I didn't like the idea of leaving her, even if it was for a few months. Now, though, after the drama of yesterday and after further reflection on the poly lifestyle, a break from her might be the best thing. Knowing she was just across campus right now made me want to march over there, sweep her into my arms, and apologize for being such an arsehole yesterday after the performance.

She never texted me back.

And I didn't blame her. I was a real bawbag about it.

If I went home, maybe I could move on from her and get my head screwed on straight. And if I was still hung up on her when I got back—well, then maybe we'd have a go at whatever this was or could be.

If she would even consider it after that fucking text.

And who knows what Poe told her. Fuck.

"Lanny, did you hear me?" my boss interrupted the self-pity train that was cruising through the station in my brain.

"Oh, sorry, sir. What was that again?"

"We have a skeleton crew heading over there early to get set up. They requested that the engineer—that would be your position—come over early as well to help with the equipment, the tech and mechanical side of things. I told Dean Terry I'd ask you what you thought. It would mean an extra two months' pay—you'd be getting a stipend on top of your usual salary, plus room and board. And we thought you might like the idea of spending the holidays with your family. You'd have two weeks off at Christmas. The other folks are going to fly back for the holidays, but you wouldn't have to if you didn't want to." He really sounded like he was trying to sell me on the idea.

"Wow, well, that sounds really generous." I took a deep breath and rubbed my hands together. "What would the new start date be?"

"It would be a week from today. If you accept, you'll fly out of Indianapolis on Saturday."

Oh, wait. Rugby. Saturday? Wow. That is soon.

"I have a rugby match on Saturday afternoon. Would I be able to fly out Saturday evening maybe or early Sunday morning?"

My boss scratched his head. "That likely wouldn't

matter as long as you got over there on Sunday sometime. So does that mean you're in?"

"When do you need to know by? I need to make sure my roommate can take care of my dog while I'm gone. I—"

"Is it a small dog?" my boss questioned. Wow, they were really desperate for me to say yes, weren't they?

"Yes, sir. She's a Scottish terrier."

A wide grin split his face. "Scottish terrier, eh? Well, sounds like she could use a visit to her native land as well. I'm sure we can make the arrangements. I just need to talk to the dean and the trip coordinator."

"Of course. Can you let me know? And I can probably give you a decision by Wednesday at the latest. Would that be okay?"

He stood up and extended his hand. "Sounds like a deal. I'll be in touch."

I shook his hand and started back to the lounge where the facilities staff took our breaks and hung out between assignments. I should have been elated. There should have been a spring in my step at the thought of getting an all-expenses-paid trip home, getting to take my dog, and also earning my regular salary plus a stipend.

But each step felt like plodding through thick mud, and my heart ached.

Despite all the overwhelming positives of taking this assignment, a big part of me was yearning for Molly.

twenty-two

. . .

molly

"SO THAT'S IT, then? I'm done?" I looked around the table at the faces of the committee members.

"That's it, you passed. Congratulations on your Master of Fine Arts!" Kat, my advisor, smiled as she and her colleagues began clapping, giving me a well-earned round of applause.

"Thank you so much for all of your guidance and support." I tried to hold back the tears stinging the corners of my eyes.

This. This was what I'd been dreaming about for years now—ever since I graduated with my bachelor's degree in English. It took me a few years of teaching high school before I realized I should have had more confidence in my ability to achieve my ultimate goal: to become a working playwright.

Now I was well on my way. And I had an idea for a new play, too.

"I heard from Allison at the Central Indiana Playhouse," Kat announced. "She was very impressed with *Scot Free*, and I anticipate she'll be calling soon to discuss details about a contract."

Pride welled up right alongside my tears. Could it be that all my dreams were coming true?

I headed home that evening and was greeted with the warm, savory smell of garlic and rosemary. Poe, Jason, Cynda, Darth and Delaney were all there with champagne, ready to toast my good news.

"What if I hadn't passed?" I asked after the first toast.

Cynda grinned. "We had absolutely every confidence in you!" She nodded, the springy black corkscrew curls on her crown bouncing in rhythm. "I couldn't imagine a world in which your brilliant play didn't wow the socks off your advisor."

Poe smirked. "Plus, I called over to the theater department's admin to check on the status. She wasn't supposed to tell me, but she made an exception."

"Well, I'm thrilled, and my advisor told me a call from Central Indiana Playhouse is imminent." I raised my glass again. "I think I'm going to need more."

"Drink up, and there's a charcuterie board on the counter," Cynda said. "Dinner should be ready in about fifteen minutes."

"I truly appreciate the effort you've all gone to in supporting me through this, and especially this crazy semester with the production," I shared with my friends. "Cynda, all of your meals were much appreciated. Poe, I could never thank you enough for finding the perfect lead for my show. Everyone else, thank you for taking care of me and picking up the slack when it came to buying groceries and cleaning the house and all that. I love and appreciate you all so much."

"We love you too!" came a chorus of voices as so many arms wrapped around me for a group hug.

This was what I loved about living in a polycule. I wasn't sure I could ever live in any other kind of configuration now that I'd experienced this. It made sense financially, emotionally, practically—on pretty much every level.

After dinner, I pulled Poe down the hallway. "Is something wrong?" she asked with an arched eyebrow.

"No, not at all, just wanted some alone time with my girlfriend. Delaney will be okay out there with those three, right?"

"Yeah, she can hold her own." Poe grinned. "So, what…you just want to make out?"

"That would be nice, but…I wanted to apologize again about what happened with Lachlan. I never wanted to make you feel like I was ashamed of you or you had to stay hidden. I know how upsetting it was and how patient you've been these past few years while I've tried to pander to my parents' expectations."

She pressed a hand to my chest and smiled. "Molly, it's okay. I'm over it now. I'm just sad that Lachlan couldn't get on the same page. But I know you connected with him and had fun, so I hope you will try dating again —dating another man or woman. Whatever floats your boat."

"I appreciate that, but I didn't drag you in here to talk about Lachlan…"

"You didn't?" Her inquisitive brow shot upward again.

"No," I grabbed both of her hands and held them tightly, looking into her sparkling hazel eyes, "I came in here to ask you a question."

"Oh? What's that?"

"I wanted to know if you'll be my date to my sister's wedding on Saturday?"

Her eyes bulged, and her mouth opened in shock. "What? Are you serious? Like a date date?"

I nodded, grinning. "I'm tired of my parents dictating my life and choices. I'm tired of hiding who I really am. If they want to disown me because I'm in love with a smart, beautiful woman, then fuck them! They don't deserve me in their lives."

"Are you serious right now?" She blinked, still not sure whether she could trust my change of heart.

"I'm totally serious. Find something nice to wear. I'm coming out to my family on Saturday, and I'm going to have the most gorgeous woman on my arm when I do."

"Oh, Molly! I'm so excited!" She leaned in and pressed her lips to my mouth, then I tangled my fingers in her long honey-colored hair, pulling her close to me so I could wrap my arms around her waist.

If I had the strength and courage to write and produce a play, I could do this.

I knew I could.

lachlan

I had two suitcases on my bed and was in the process of emptying out my drawers and closet when Darth came home. Bonnie did her obligatory bark and bolted to him for the little bit of attention he bestowed upon her when he came home. I was glad my boss had pulled some strings so I could take her with me to Scotland. I really didn't want to leave her with Darth. I was sure he would take care of her, but he couldn't love her like her daddy did.

I was shocked to see him crouch down and allow her to

snuggle up to him while he stroked his hands down her fur. "Hey, girl, good to see you. Did you miss me today? Did you have a good day?"

I stood in the hallway, trying to keep my mouth from dropping open. "Wow, you're in a good mood."

He smiled, which was also not typical for him. "Yeah, had a good day. Just got back from Cynda and Jason's, and she made dinner. We were celebrating—" He stopped abruptly and waved his hand.

"Celebrating what?"

"Oh, never mind, you don't want to hear about that." He walked toward me to get to his room, and I backed down the hall, stopping in front of the door to my room.

"Hear about what? Just tell me." I pursed my lips as I stared at him. He sure was acting strange.

"Molly's play. She passed and is getting her master's degree. I guess she has you in part to thank for that, huh?" He stood there, looking into my room at the suitcases on the bed. "Going somewhere?"

I straightened my shoulders, trying not to dwell too much on what he'd said about Molly. "Yeah, actually, leaving for Scotland on Saturday after my rugby match."

"Scotland?" he repeated, seeming confused.

"Yeah, you know, where I'm from?" My eyes narrowed at him as I tried to figure out how he could be so clueless sometimes.

"Wow, were you gonna tell me you're leaving?" He backed up a few feet, and I noticed his fists had clenched at his side.

"I'm still gonna pay my rent, and I'm taking Bonnie Skye with me. So, it shouldn't affect you at all. I'll be back in May, anyway. Well, more than likely."

His head cocked, his dark eyes drilling into me. "But I

was planning to move in with Cynda and Jason. I was going to sublet my room here—"

I held my hands up. "You're the one whose name is on the lease. You'll have to figure it out. But I'm planning to come back in May. If that doesn't end up happening, I'll give plenty of notice and will keep paying until our lease renews which isn't until August," I promised.

He shook his head. "Why are you going, though? I thought you and Molly were—"

I sucked in a deep breath. Why did her name keep coming off his tongue? "Weren't you here when Poe came by the other morning? You heard what she said, that Molly was trying to appease her family by dating a man."

Darth's nostrils flared. He was always completely oblivious to everyone and everything around him, but then he said, "That's not what I heard."

"It's not?" I crossed my arms over my chest.

"No, I heard that Poe was hurt because Molly dating a man meant she *could* appease her family. Not that Molly was dating you because she was trying to appease anybody. I know she cares about you, and you care about her."

Had Darth been the victim of body-snatching or some-thing? I couldn't believe the words coming out of his mouth. Aliens had abducted him and reprogrammed him. Surely. That was the only explanation.

"You were just over there, right?" I fired back.

He nodded.

"Did she say anything about me?"

Darth appeared to think for a moment. "Well, no, but—"

"See?" I stormed back into my room and continued violently tossing clothes into one of the suitcases. It turned out that slamming down a lightweight cotton t-shirt was not as gratifying as something with a little heft might have been. *Och.*

He held his hands up and backed away some more. "Forget I said anything."

I would forget.

By the time my soul reconnected with my bonnie homeland, Molly would be a distant memory.

At least that was the plan.

molly

If everything was going so well, and I was so happy to be finished with grad school, then why did my mind keep replaying every single moment I'd spent with Lachlan?

And we'd spent a lot of time together, so there was an endless loop of memories cycling in there.

Later that night, after Darth and Delaney left, I told Poe, Cynda and Jason that I was sorry things hadn't worked out with Lachlan, but he just wasn't ready for a poly relationship. Maybe he never would be. And that was okay. Polyamory wasn't for everybody.

That was the conclusion I'd drawn when Poe finally told me about her visit to his house. I wasn't pleased she'd gone over there without my knowledge, but her heart was in the right place. She was a problem solver by nature, and she thought talking to him would solve a problem. Polyamory is all about communication. If we were going to have the kitchen table poly dynamic we'd established with Jason, Cynda, and now Darth and Delaney, then Lachlan needed to be able to communicate with his metamour.

If he ended up dating someone else, I'd need to get

along with that person too. Open communication and respect were vital to a successful poly relationship, whether it was a vee, like this one, or a triad or whatever configuration.

Maybe I hadn't spent enough time educating him on the finer points and etiquette. We were pretty caught up in two things: the play and fucking each other. I had to admit, I was going to miss the latter very much.

But I'd get over him, right?

Sure, I would. And once I came out to my parents about being both bi and poly, I wouldn't have to worry about my secret coming out in our small town. All my cards would be out on the table.

Just as they should have been all along.

It was just that I wanted Lachlan at that table too.

twenty-three

· · ·

lachlan

I PLAYED extra hard at our match today, and we came out on top. All the usual suspects congratulated me when I was crowned Man of the Match once again.

I raised my glass to everyone in the bar. "This is my last game of the season. Thanks for making it a good one today. I'll be back next fall! Cheers, lads!"

I outdrank my counterpart from the other team once again. I had never lost that challenge. Pretty sure my Scottish heritage wouldn't allow me to.

"What's this about it being your last game?" Sam elbowed me as I set my glass down on the bar top. It was replaced with a fresh beer within seconds. "Where ya going?"

"I'm going to Scotland—leaving tonight, in fact." I took a sip from the new glass.

Sam's thick eyebrows shot up his face. "What? Why? Are you coming back?"

"Relax, it's probably not permanent. I got a great

temporary job offer over there, and it sounds like it will be cake. So, I'll be there for about six months. Unless I find a bonnie lass over there and decide to stay." I chuckled deep in my chest, trying to make myself believe that was possible when I hadn't stopped thinking about Molly. I couldn't believe it had been almost a week since I'd seen her, and she hadn't texted me once.

She had Poe. She didn't need me.

"Well, we'll sure miss you out on the pitch," Kevin said as he joined us. He must have been eavesdropping on the conversation. Not that it was private.

"Aye, you'll miss me 'cause you'll be losing a lot of games," I joked, raising my fresh pint of beer to my mates.

"Lachlan?" a soft feminine voice sounded behind me.

I turned around to see Molly's housemate, Cynda, standing there with her boyfriend, Jason, and my roommate, Darth.

"Hey, everyone, you're out and about this Saturday, eh?" I took a swig of my beer.

"Did you say something about leaving?" Cynda stepped a little closer to me, flanked on either side by her two guys.

"Aye, didn't Darth tell ya? He'll have an empty house for a few months if he moves in with you. I'll be gone about six months, working for the biology department as they do some research on Highland coos."

"That sounds like a great opportunity," Cynda said. "Does Molly know you're leaving?"

I shook my head. "No, we're not really talking now that the play is done. No need to, I reckon."

She cocked her head and looked at me with her brown doe eyes. I noticed neither of her two men were saying a word, content to let her do all the talking. "I'm pretty sure you two need to have a conversation."

What was this woman's problem? Did she think she had ESP or something?

"Well, I'm leaving in a few hours to head to the airport." I put my empty glass on the counter. When the bartender grabbed it to refill it, I waved him off.

"I think you'll regret not talking to her before you go," she said. "She's at her sister's wedding today, but you could text her. Ask her to give you a call when she has a moment."

I swallowed hard. Why did her words sound like a prophecy?

She stared at me for a moment, then her lips spread into a wide smile. "I'm an empath," she explained. "I feel vibrations from you, and I have from her, and I know you have unfinished business."

"*Och*, that's thoughtful of you, and I don't wanna be rude, but maybe butt out now, aye?" My eyes left her face for just a second to catch the expression on Darth's, which looked like one of warning.

Before I could say anything else, my phone started vibrating in my pocket. It was likely the coordinator for the research trip checking in. "Sorry, I gotta take this. Have a good day."

As I stepped away, I heard Cynda *tsk*. "You'll regret it if you don't at least say goodbye to her."

molly

Today had been…not at all what I expected.

Poe and I showed up at the church at noon, which was when we were supposed to be there for photos. I figured

Meredith had enough people helping her get ready that she didn't need me in the way.

My mother was the first person I saw. She was scurrying around looking for a safety pin to hold somebody's dress.

"Oh, hey, Mrs. Rose, I have one," Poe offered. She carried a veritable convenience store strapped to her shoulder. The sheer volume of odds and ends in her purse was mesmerizing.

My mother stopped short. "Oh. I'm glad you made it, Molly. I thought you were bringing a date?"

Poe pulled a safety pin from her purse at the same time I said, "I did bring a date. This is her. And I need you and the rest of the family to understand something very important: she's not just my roommate, she's my girlfriend."

My mother hardly batted an eye. "I'm glad you're here, Poe, and you just saved the day! One of the bridesmaid's dresses is showing a little too much, if you know what I mean."

Poe politely nodded. "You're welcome."

"Well, come on, Molly, we need to get going. The photographer is waiting. Your dress looks nice." My mother turned to leave, and it was apparent she hadn't heard a word I said.

"Mom, did you hear me?"

Poe clutched my arm and shook her head. "Not now," she mouthed. "Let her go."

I rolled my eyes and grabbed Poe's hand. Well, I wasn't going to act like she was just my roommate any longer. We walked hand in hand down the hall and into the sanctuary, which was filled with fresh flowers and candles. The heady scent of roses hung in the air as I adjusted the strap on my silky burgundy gown.

"Do I look alright?" I asked my date.

She leaned forward and pressed a kiss to my forward. "You look absolutely stunning."

"Got it!" someone exclaimed, and I looked up to find a photographer aiming a camera right toward us.

I shook off the effect of the flash, which had startled me. "Oh, hi."

That gained the attention of everyone else in the room. My sister came rushing toward me in her bridal gown, all glowing lace, tiny pearls, and sequins. She threw her arms around me. "You look absolutely beautiful," she gushed.

"Wait, don't ruin your hair or makeup," I warned, stepping back. "Let me look at you."

My gaze trailed up and down her figure, perfectly encased in her strapless sweetheart neckline dress with its ballgown skirt and train. Her veil was attached to a delicate pearl and rhinestone tiara with dark curls piled on top of her head and a few tendrils framing her face.

"You're breathtaking." I took her hands in mine and squeezed them. "I'm so very happy for you. Eli looks great too!" I waved over to my future brother-in-law, who was standing in a small group with his groomsmen and best man. He and my dad walked over, and the photographer snapped a few more photos.

"Where's Lachlan?" Meredith wondered, looking around the sanctuary. "Isn't he here? I wanted to make sure the photographer got a pic of him in his kilt."

"He's not coming," I announced.

All of the chattering taking place between the other bridesmaids, the groomsmen, and various other plus-ones and family members standing around came to an abrupt halt.

I was going to try this announcement again.

"Lachlan won't be here to celebrate with us as he's on his way to Scotland today. I have brought my girlfriend, Poe, and I'm very happy and proud to have her on my arm tonight." I turned to her, extended my arm, and waited for her to come to my side. Then I wrapped my arm around her and pulled her to me in an affectionate squeeze. "I don't want to disrupt Meredith's wedding, or take any attention off her and Eli, but I need you all to understand that I'm bisexual, I'm polyamorous, and I'm not going to hide anymore. I will not be taking questions at this time."

It was so quiet, I could have sworn I heard the clock ticking at the back of the sanctuary. My father had it placed there so, when he was preaching, he could make sure he wasn't getting too long-winded. He couldn't trust himself to remember to look at his watch.

My gaze bounced around the room, stopping on each face to see the expressions there. To my surprise, no one looked shocked. No one looked angry. Even my mother continued to wear a smile. Maybe the happiness of Meredith and Eli's special day was enough to override any disappointment my announcement might cause.

Finally, Meredith broke the silence. "Molly, I've known Poe wasn't just your roommate since you very first introduced her to us. I don't care who you love, sis. I love you just the way you are."

I was so surprised, so astounded by this declaration that I just stood there frozen for a moment, and then my father spoke.

"Your mother and I love you unconditionally, Molly. We always have, and we always will. We want the same thing for you as we want for Meredith: for you to be happy and healthy and to spend your life doing what you love with whoever you love. That's it." He stretched out his arms, and I thought I might die.

Before I could stop them, tears were rolling down my cheeks as his arms wrapped around me. I went straight from his arms to my mother's.

And somehow, I was standing there in my father's church, and instead of lightning striking me or being disowned, I was being accepted and loved just the way God made me.

We finished up with photos, and Poe pulled me aside. "You're sure you're okay?"

I smiled. "Of course I am. That went way better than I could have ever hoped for." I took her hand into mine. "I'm so glad I finally got the courage to come out to them. I just wish I'd done it sooner. I should have had more faith in them."

"What's this about Lachlan going to Scotland?" Poe questioned. "How did you know?"

"Darth told me," I said.

My girlfriend's mouth dropped open. "Darth? The same Darth we know? The completely unaware and clueless guy my brother and Cynda are dating?"

I laughed at her apt description. "Yeah, I know. I was shocked as well."

"When did he tell you?" Her hazel eyes bounced between mine.

I squeezed her hand. "Last night when he was over. I think you were helping Cynda in the kitchen, and Jason had gone to the restroom."

"Why didn't you tell me?" Poe demanded.

I shrugged. "I'm trying not to think about him. I'm still hurt by what happened, that he didn't give us more of a chance."

"He's going to Scotland permanently?" She blinked rapidly.

"He has a job offer there," I explained. "I'm surprised you didn't know because it's a team of researchers from the bio department going to study Highland cattle."

"Oh!" she exclaimed. "He's going on that trip? I thought it didn't start until January?"

I shrugged. "I guess he's going over early. Probably to see his family and stuff. Maybe he won't come back." Those words had been swirling in my mind for days, but saying them out loud was a stab to my heart.

Poe's eyes locked on mine. "You miss him, don't you?"

I sighed. "Well, of course I do, but I guess it wasn't meant to be."

"Why did Darth tell you?"

"He thought I should give him a call. But why would I do that when he's leaving the country?" Looking down at my feet, I was starting to regret these heels. I missed my combat boots. "What if he doesn't want to come back?"

Poe stroked a finger down my cheek. "He'll come back. I'm sure he misses you too."

I shook my head. "I just don't think we were meant to be..."

I didn't get a chance to tell her that my heart hurt because he'd stolen a piece of it. A part of me was getting on that plane with him, and he would carry it with him to the Highlands.

My mother appeared out of nowhere and told me I needed to come back to the room where my sister and her other bridesmaids were gathered. It was almost time to walk down the aisle.

Poe smiled and gave me a wave as I turned to leave with my mother. I looked back over my shoulder before we turned down the hall. She had taken out her phone and had it pressed to her ear.

twenty-four

. . .

lachlan

I HAD everything ready to be loaded into the truck. The plan was to take Bonnie out one more time, then I'd coax her with a treat into her crate, already anchored in the truck, and we'd be on our way to the airport. But before I could get her back inside, Darth came running out of the house holding my kilt in his arms.

"*Och, dinnae need that,*" I chuckled at his helpful gesture, "plenty more where that'un came from!"

"No," he shook his head, "not for you to pack. For you to wear. Right now."

"What? I'm not wearing a kilt to the airport."

"I just got off the phone. Come inside. You need to get ready."

"What are ya goin' on about?"

"What time does your flight leave?"

"Not till midnight, but I gotta get there, check myself and my lassie here in, and—"

"You've got time. C'mon."

molly

"What's going on? You seem really distracted?" I had my arms around Poe's waist, and we were dancing under the disco ball. Meredith's wedding reception was half over, and though I was still thinking about Lachlan and getting a little misty-eyed from time to time between that and my baby sister getting hitched, over all, I was still in awe of my family's acceptance of my little coming out speech earlier.

"I'm fine, sorry." Poe swirled us closer to the bridal table, where Meredith shot us both a huge smile and a thumbs-up. "There are just a lot of people staring at us is all."

"Yeah, well, most of my parents' church is here," I explained. "I bet my dad is going to be bombarded with questions at the worship service tomorrow morning."

She sighed. "What do you think he'll say?"

I shrugged. "I have no idea. But hopefully it will change some hearts and minds among his congregation—maybe they'll all become a little more accepting of LGBT folks?"

"That would be a really positive thing to come out of all this." She grinned and gestured between us.

Then a funny thing happened. She cleared her throat and spun me around so fast, I nearly lost my breath.

When she stopped, a voice cut through the fog of one too many glasses of wine, "May I cut in?"

Standing there in the shimmering disco lights was none other than Lachlan, looking so tall and handsome in his kilt. I would have probably fallen over right there on the dance floor if Poe hadn't propped me up.

"What are you doing here?" I choked out. "I thought you were going to Scotland?"

"I wanted a dance with you first," was all he said.

"Just one dance?" I pinned my eyes to his. The dance floor lights made them flash silver.

Poe stepped away, a smile on her face. "Enjoy, you two."

He opened his arms, and I stepped into them. "I'll take whatever you'll give me," he admitted as he wrapped those thick, beefy limbs around me.

My gaze never left his. "I can't believe you were going to leave without saying goodbye."

He sighed, his chest heaving so hard, it caused a shudder through his whole body. "Well, all your friends called me on it. Between Cynda, Darth, and Poe, they all convinced me I was making a terrible mistake."

"Huh, well, it's good to have your polycule watching out for you." I couldn't hide my smile as my gaze shot over to Poe. She was talking to one of my sister's brides-maids, but she flashed me a wink as soon as we made eye contact.

He cocked his head. "If that's what being poly is about —having a family who watches out for you—"

I gave him a vigorous nod. "That's exactly what it is!"

His masculine scent seeped into my nostrils as he twirled me around. *God, he smells so damn good.* "Well, then maybe I need to give it a shot?"

"But you're going to Scotland..." I knew it was only temporary...but six months was a long time.

"Come with me, Molly. Come to Scotland with me— just for two weeks. I'll get the lab equipment set up, and I'll help the researchers find someone local to work with them. My brother Finn is an engineer—I'm sure he has a lad or two who can help."

Shock made me blink several times in rapid succession. "Seriously?"

"Poe encouraged me to ask you to come with me," he confessed. "Call it a graduation present. You're done with school, right?"

"I have a paper to write for my final class, but, other than that—"

"Well, the scenery in the Highlands is *very* inspiring…"

My head was spinning. "When do we need to leave?"

He grinned. "I changed my flight to tomorrow, and I know there's at least one more seat on the plane—"

I couldn't believe this was happening. My heart felt like it was going to explode, it was so full right now. Between finishing my master's degree, getting my family's blessing, and now Lachlan wanting to give us a shot—I felt like a hot air balloon. Like I might just float away on sheer joy.

Thankfully, those big, strong arms tightened around me, anchoring me to the ground. Then a pair of full, luscious lips brushed against mine, whispering, "Say aye, lassie…"

"Aye, Lach—" His lips claimed mine before I could finish his name.

As he spun me around the dance floor, I'd never felt so happy, so free.

I wrote a play called *Scot Free*, but my heart was full of one particular Scot.

And I wouldn't have it any other way.

epilogue

. . .

lachlan

SCOTLAND WAS everything I could have dreamed of and more. I introduced my family to Molly and Bonnie Skye, I reconnected with old friends, and I helped the research group from IU get set up in the little town of Plockton near Isle of Skye.

Then I got to show my lovely lassies the beauty of my homeland. It was raining, and the mist was so thick on our way across the bridge to Skye, we could barely see the water or the mountains.

"I'm sure this would be beautiful if it wasn't so cloudy," she commented as our car snaked around a narrow one-lane bend.

"We're almost to the Old Man of Storr. Remember seeing it in my scrapbook?" I drove a little farther and then pulled off in the car park. "Here we are."

We both got out of the car and stood facing the mountains. Fog hung so low that none of the rock formations were visible. When I set Bonnie on the ground, she strolled over to sniff the grass near the bumper. "The best view is from the trail anyway."

Molly cocked her head, and those green eyes lasered into me. "Are you sure it's going to be worth it to hike all the way up there?"

"Aye, it's dreich today, but yeh wanted tae see the spot where that photo of me and my brothers was taken when I was a wee lad, dinnae yeh?" I reached out to take her hand.

She huffed. "Fine, but if I hike all the way up there, and we can't see shit, you owe me an hour of oral to make up for it. And a foot rub."

I chuckled. "Lassie, I'll gladly give yeh both of those things either way."

A melodic giggle flowed out of her lips as she smiled up at me. "Okay, my sexy Scot, lead the way."

She complained once or twice on the hike to the top of the hill. There were a couple of steep spots, and I had to pick Bonnie up and carry her a few times. But as soon as we made it to the top, where the Old Man of Storr and his companions proudly jutted up into the sky like sentinels guarding the shoreline, the thick clouds parted. The mist was burned off by the persistent sun beaming down, just as snowflakes began to swirl in the air, giving the light a magical sparkling effect.

"Oh my god!" she gasped when she noticed the view went all the way to the ocean. The remaining clouds sailed by, revealing a rainbow arching toward an island perched on the horizon. "Oh my god, Lachlan, look!"

I let her stand there for a moment, taking it all in. It was a view that would steal your breath if you weren't careful. And when she'd drunk her fill, I stood behind her, wrapping my arms around her waist and resting my chin on her shoulder as Bonnie Skye sat obediently beside us.

She turned in my arms, those green eyes staring up at me with tears and wonder. "It's even more beautiful than your photos."

"Aye, nae way to capture the true beauty of my homeland." I nodded, and as one of the tears began to slip down her face, I brushed it away with my thumb.

"How can you ever leave this place?" she wondered. "I understand why you left it before, but how could you leave it again?"

"Easy," I said, "my love lives in a wee place called Bloomington, Indiana."

Her smile saturated her entire face, and her green eyes glowed with joy. "I guess we can always come visit your home."

I took her hands into mine and pulled her so close, my words brushed her lips, "My home is where you are, lassie."

molly

A year ago, I thought I'd be looking for apartments in New York at the start of the new year. Instead, I found myself loading up furniture into a truck whose destination is the other side of town.

A year ago, I thought I'd be waiting tables while I also waited for some producer to fall in love with my play. Instead, we start casting for *Scot Free* at the Central Indiana Playhouse next week. I've been hired on as a consultant, and I will be commuting to the theater in Indianapolis a few days a week.

A year ago, I thought Poe and I would have to keep our

relationship under wraps until we were settled in New York and had spent all of my trust fund money. Instead, the money is in the bank, and my parents offered to help us move all of our stuff to Lachlan's house. Delaney will be moving in with us too, while Darth is moving in with Cynda and Jason.

A year ago, Lachlan thought he would never put his art and philosophy degrees to use, but he'd been hired to design the sets for a certain new play debuting this season at the Central Indiana Playhouse. He'd also applied to a certain MFA program at a certain midwestern university that I may or may not be intimately familiar with. If he's accepted—and I know he will be—he'll start in the fall semester.

Before we leave Cynda and Jason's house, I gather my polycule in the living room.

"I don't even know where to start." I look around the room at everyone's faces: Lachlan, Poe, Cynda, Jason, Darth and Delaney. Plus two new faces: Aris and Noah, Cynda's friends who will be moving into my old room.

"Between Poe convincing me to cast Lachlan in the play; all of you playing matchmaker; and Cynda, Poe and Darth all conspiring to bring us together at the last possible moment—I don't know how words can fail me when I'm a writer, but they are right now. I love you all so much. When I tried to explain to Lachlan why belonging to a polycule is so amazing, I found I didn't have to— because he saw for himself how we love each other and look out for each other. He saw how we are family, and he decided he wants that too. I know we're moving across town, but you'll always be my family. And I will always love you all. Even you, Darth."

I can tell Darth is trying to think of a smart-ass retort,

but instead, he just joins the massive group hug happening right here in our living room.

Former living room, that is.

In a few minutes, I'll be walking into Lachlan's house with Poe and Delaney, and we'll have our own little polycule branch on the east side of town. And we'd be starting our journey with seeing how Sagan and Bonnie Skye get on with each other.

Hopefully, that will be the only drama our polycule will face in our new life together.

After all, love and drama often go hand in hand.

But love always wins in the end.

Continue the love in the next PolyAm Fam book!
Books2read.com/PolyAmFam2

Join Phoebe's newsletter here: bit.ly/
PhoebeAlexanderNews

Join my reader group for sneak peeks and giveaways:
Phoebes Angels

about the author

USA Today Bestselling Author Phoebe Alexander writes sexpositive, bodypositive erotic romance featuring compelling plots intertwined with passionate, fiery encounters. She believes that real, relatable characters can have even steamier sex than billionaires, rock stars, and the young and lithe-bodied. She also advocates for ethical non-monogamy through her writing.

Phoebe lives on the East Coast of the US with her husband, sons, and multiple fur babies. When she's not writing, she works as an editor and consultant for indie authors. She also volunteers her time running a 6000-member indie author support group. Her sexual fantasies have all been fulfilled, and now her single greatest fantasy is just having some damn free time.

facebook.com / phoebealexanderauthor
instagram.com / authorphoebealexander
bookbub.com / authors / phoebe-alexander
tiktok.com / @authorphoebealexander

also by phoebe alexander

Mountains Series

Mountains Wanted

Mountains Climbed

Mountains Loved

Christmas in the Mountains

The Navigator

The Explorer

The Adventurer

Mountains Transcended

Eastern Shore Swingers Series

Fisher of Men

The Catch

Siren Call

Sailors Knot

Turning the Tide

Spicetopia Series

Penny & Pryce

Sugar & Spice

Virtue & Vice

Fire & Ice

Naughty & Nice

Dares & Dice

Loyalty & Lies

Spice Up Our Marriage Series

Project Paradise

Rule Breaker

The Playground

Keeping Secrets

Alpha Bet Guys Series

A Hole

The Big O

Need the D

Hard F

Ride the C

Polyam Fam

The Scottish Play

Break a Leg

Standalones

Authority Issues

Clean Grammar for Dirty Minds

www.ingramcontent.com/pod-product-compliance
Lightning Source LLC
Chambersburg PA
CBHW061806190726

48289CB00007B/2089